CONFLICT IN THE CLUB

CONFLICT IN THE CLUB

PHILIP M. COHEN

LUMINARE PRESS
WWW.LUMINAREPRESS.COM

Conflict in the Club
Copyright © 2024 by Philip M. Cohen

All rights reserved. This book or any portion thereof may not be reproduced or used in any manner whatsoever without the express written permission of the publisher, except for the use of brief quotations in a book review.

Printed in the United States of America

Luminare Press
442 Charnelton St.
Eugene, OR 97401
www.luminarepress.com

LCCN: 2023920381
ISBN: 979-8-88679-416-8

*To Sarah and Nancy,
the newest members of the clan.
Thank you to Julia Wayne for your
thoughtful and inspired editing.*

PROLOGUE

"Put your hand right there, luv. Yeah, that's it."

Rog loved these weekend nights at the club. He was usually able to get a semi-big name in the place, which generated decent publicity, which brought out a bigger than usual crowd, which brought out so many young lovelies. Such as this little red-haired doll hanging over him from behind and snaking her hand down his chest, inching her way past his stomach.

"Aah, that's nice," he sighed, as he snuggled his grizzled, white stubbled face into her flawless young neck.

He could only imagine what it must have been like in the old days, the 60's, 70's, even the 80's and 90's. When the biggest rockers in the world would clamor to be on this very stage, visible right through the one-way window in his office. The audience enthusiasm would boil over with emotional displays of all sorts. Chicks stripping off their tee shirts for their favorite bands, sex backstage, smoking, snorting, shooting in the bathrooms. When "anything goes" was the motto of the place and not a history lesson of the way things were on the Sunset Strip. For what it's worth, my ass. These days you have to promise people baked nostalgia in the form of some band that should have given it up long ago (yeah, you, Climax Blues Band) to get anyone down here. But at least they drew a decent crowd.

"Ow! Not your teeth, ya useless tramp!" Rog pushed her away, rubbed his marked neck and adjusted his pants.

"Oh, I'm sorry, Rog," said the teenager, 5' 2", no more than 100 pounds, dressed in a ripped jeans miniskirt, white tee shirt with strategically placed holes and red platform shoes. "Ya think I can have some blow?" She smiled and batted her eyes in her best approximation of alluring.

"Yeah, yeah, sure" sighed Rog, easing his chair from the desk, opening the top drawer and finding a thin glass tube. He poured out a small amount of white powder in a mound and handed the girl a tiny gold spoon, a real relic of the glory days. Maybe he was getting too old for this, he thought. He'd been managing the club for five years now and had the white hair to show for it. A British ex-pat, in his late forties, slightly overweight, but muscular, he relished being the king of this castle. Where else could he have final say over the doings of a place like this? Not that the salary was so great. But there were the added benefits, he thought as he watched the beautiful girl make short work of the powder. What was her name? Jenny?

"Bang, bang, bang!" Someone was knocking hard on the door and a moment later it swung open. Johnny Whoops, a singer/guitarist in a local band, bolted into the room.

"Rog," Johnny said urgently. "You gotta get down to the front, man. Something's going on."

Rog stood, shoved the girl aside and brushed past Johnny on his way down the stairs.

"Where's Tim?" he asked, referring to the huge Samoan bouncer always stationed in the front of the club. He bounded down the steps, pushing aside people staring at the four musicians playing on stage. He didn't wait for an answer as he pushed through the crowd, ignoring the band and everything else, his eyes on the front entrance.

He stepped to the front door and heard Tim in a shouting match with at least two other guys. Rog turned the corner and Tim, all three hundred plus pounds of him, was trying to fend off two long haired biker types nearly in Tim's weight bracket. They were in the bouncer's face, yelling, threatening him, gesturing wildly. A crowd surrounded them in a semi-circle, frightened and fascinated.

"Hold up here, wha's the…" was all Rog could get out before he found himself being lifted off the ground and flying through the air. He slammed into the brick wall face of the club and heard a sickening crunch. Only a microsecond lapsed before Rog felt a mind numbing pain from his right side, hip through foot. He passed out.

CHAPTER 1

The morning light streaming through the apartment window woke Shirlee Shore. She opened her pearl blue eyes in a squint, trying to focus on the new day. It had been a long night, an awful night and she needed coffee before she could do anything. She reached out her left hand and poked the body lying next to her.

"Baby…" Shirlee pleaded. "Coffee, please." She turned on her side, curling her arm around the body sleeping on his side. She tightened her grip, trying to pull him awake.

"Whhaa…?" groaned Johnny "Whoops" Watson, clutching Shirlee's arm and pressing it to his chest. "Get me some coffee," he mumbled, unable to open his eyes.

"You!" Shirlee shoved Johnny, trying to push him off the bed and all the way into the kitchen. She didn't succeed, but he was now awake. He turned to her, pulled her close and kissed her long and intensely.

"Hmmm," she murmured. "That's nice. Almost as good as coffee."

"All right, all right. You're no fun." Johnny shifted his legs onto the floor, stood and walked in his boxers into the kitchen. Just under six feet, wiry and fit, at 26 years old he was able to recover from most wild nights on the town. And last night was one of those, for sure, he thought. He poured hot water from the tap into a couple of mugs, added instant coffee, stirred them and brought them back to the bedroom, handing a mug to Shirlee.

"Yes, thanks," said Shirlee, sitting up and eagerly taking her first sip. She shook her head, her pixie cut black dyed hair bouncing in response. "Woo, that was crazed last night, huh? Poor Rog."

"Yeah," agreed Johnny. He had followed Rog out the door of the club and been part of the chaos that followed. Tim and the bikers about to throw down and suddenly Rog was crumpled against the wall, people screaming, running in all directions. The West Hollywood Sheriffs had arrived and questioned everyone on the scene. But to Johnny it seemed like chaos. All he could tell the cops was that some biker had thrown Rog against the wall like a rag doll. "We oughta visit him at Cedars."

"Let's go this afternoon. I have to be at the dump for the early evening shift."

"All right. I'll call Billy and see if he and Olivia want to go. Then we can drop you back on Ventura at the restaurant." Johnny reached for his phone and speed dialed Billy Bates' number. After half a ring, Billy's voice came on the line.

"Hey, bro mahn. How's it hangin'?" Billy's Jamaican patois by way of the Valley slithered out.

"Yeah, OK, Billy. Ya hear about Rog?" Johnny explained what happened at the club last night and his and Shirlee's plan for today. "You and Livie wanna come with?"

"Ya sure. I'll swing by in Harry's heap in an hour," Billy said, referencing the battered Subaru SUV that Olivia had inherited from her late cousin Harry. "Mahn, I'm lovin Sundays. A full day without work. See ya soon."

"Right. Bye." Johnny disconnected the phone and reached for his pants, stripped off and discarded in an exhausted haze late the night before. "Hey, baby," he called. "We got anything to eat?"

CHAPTER 2

"John! Shirl! Come down!"

A window opened on the second floor of the five story apartment building and Johnny's head appeared.

"Hang on, Billy. We'll be right down," he said. "You ready?" he asked Shirlee, who was putting the finishing touches on the black mascara around her eyes.

"All set. Work for you?"

Johnny grinned and opened the apartment door. They exited, went down in the elevator and joined Billy outside the building. The brown Subaru SUV was parked at the curb and a quintessential California blonde was seated in the passenger seat. Billy hopped behind the wheel, while Johnny opened the side door of the SUV. He and Shirlee climbed in.

"Hey guys," the blonde girl said. "How's it going?"

"Hi Livie," said Shirlee, reaching over and kissing Olivia on the cheek before sitting behind her in the bench seat next to Johnny.

"So f'd up about Rog," continued Olivia. "Weren't you guys there? What happened?"

Billy pulled away from the curb toward Van Nuys Boulevard, made a right and headed south toward the freeway.

"Not really sure," answered Johnny. "It looked like a run of the mill fight in front of the club until Rog got out there. Then all hell broke loose."

"I hope he's okay," said Olivia. "He's been so good to us."

"Yeah," agreed Billy. "Not ev'ry man'ger let a bunch a deadbeats like us jam a 'is club."

Johnny snorted a bemused laugh. But Billy was right. Rog had booked their band, Conflict, into his historic club on a fairly regular basis in the past six months, helping them grow an audience from a couple of dozen people to a healthy friends list. Plus Olivia joining the group had become a bonus attraction. Her raw but spirited drumming had lifted the music to a new level. And her looks certainly kept the male eyes in any audience fixed on the stage. It was such a nice turnaround, thought Johnny, after the tragic loss last year of Harry, their number one fan, friend and, in Olivia's case, cousin.

A half hour later, having steered the SUV in Sunday light traffic onto the Ventura Freeway, off Laurel Canyon and through the storied hills into Hollywood, Billy pulled into the visitor's parking lot at Cedars-Sinai Hospital. The sprawling medical facility was situated off Beverly Boulevard in West Hollywood, a separate governmental entity and at times a different world than the city of Los Angeles.

After checking with the front desk, the four friends made their way to the room Rog was sharing with another patient on the fifth floor west. The antiseptic smell of ammonia permeated the air as they walked past a man in his mid-twenties stretched out in the bed nearest the door, watching a football game on the TV above him, his right shoulder and arm in a cast.

Johnny thought he looked uncomfortable but those thoughts vanished once he saw Rog. His mane of white hair spread over the pillow, Rog's eyes were half closed. The right side of his round face was bruised purple and a gauze pad covered his jaw. The left half of his body was under the hospital blankets, leaving the right side visible. A half body cast ran from Rog's hip to his ankle. In his right arm was an I.V., dripping fluid from the transparent bags hanging in stands next to the bed.

Shirlee moved to the left side of the bed, touching Rog's shoulder. The others crowded around.

"Rog? Rog, you awake?" said Shirlee in a voice only slightly louder than a whisper. She squeezed his shoulder gently.

Rog's eyelids fluttered slightly and a murmur rose from his throat.

"Rog?" said Johnny, "Rog, can you hear me?"

"He's on so much oxycodone, he's lucky if he hears anything," said a nurse entering the room. She was five five, brown hair in a blue nurse's uniform with a name tag over her right breast that read "Appel." "Give me some room here." She wedged beside Johnny, checked the IV lines and monitors, took Rog's pulse and straightened his blankets.

"Uh, umm," Rog stirred from the activity and opened his left eye wider. "That you, Johnny?" he mumbled. "Wha happened?"

"Hey, Rog," said Johnny. He moved closer. "You're in the hospital. How ya feelin'?"

"Yeah, I'...m fi...ne," Rog said, drawing out the words as he began to drift off.

"Come on, Johnny," said Shirlee. "We'll visit again soon," she said to Rog as she edged toward the door. Billy, Olivia and Johnny turned to follow.

"Give him a day or two," said Nurse Appel. She left the room and turned toward the nurses' station.

The four friends exited the room when a yelp came from Rog's room. Johnny went back to his bedside. Rog wiggled his fingers, urging Johnny closer. He bent down and Rog whispered in his ear "Players." Johnny looked at Rog not understanding but Rog couldn't explain further. He had again faded away from the influence of the drugs.

"Wha d'he say?" Billy asked Johnny as they, Olivia and Shirlee exited the hospital doors.

"Players," said Johnny. "All he said was 'Players.' "

"Wha that mean?"

"Damn if I know. Maybe it didn't mean anything and he was in an oxy dream." Johnny reached down and opened the passenger side of the SUV as the friends piled in. Players, he thought. Maybe nothing. But something about the word sounded familiar and the urgency of Rog's whisper had imprinted itself in his mind.

CHAPTER 3

Monday morning and Shirlee was alone in the apartment. Johnny had left an hour earlier for work at the bank in Beverly Hills. He looked so good in that uniform, thought Shirlee. Almost made up for that lowly security guard pay.

She gazed out the window to the corner of Van Nuys Boulevard, traffic having thinned after the early morning and before the midday rush. A brief respite when the noise wasn't quite so bad and you could imagine taking a walk to the park on Victory Boulevard. Well, I do have the early evening shift at Norm's tonight, she thought. Time for some fresh air.

She shed her nightshirt, Johnny's Iron Maiden tee, and slipped on a plain yellow blouse and jeans. She admired herself in the mirror, all whippet thin 5' four of her, happy she could look good in Levi's. Not that they could afford better. Someday. Stepping into a pair of beige Van's, she scooped up her house keys and headed for the front door when the door buzzer from downstairs went off.

She pressed the button to answer. "Hello?"
"Shirlee? Is that you? It's Charles."
"Charles? What are you doing here?"
"I have to talk to you. Can I come up?"

"I'm coming down. Be there in a second." What was he doing here? Charles was a regular at Johnny's gigs at clubs around town, always dressed in unique clothes, ready to party, eager to be part of the scene. As far as Shirlee could recall, the only time he had been at their apartment was after a job they had at a nearby club called Paulie's Place. Usually a heavy metal cover band spot, the manager, a guy with a Lemmy-like bushy moustache and a matching cowboy hat, had hired Johnny and Conflict not realizing that they play almost all original tunes. After three songs Semi-Lemmy, as the band called him, pulled the plug and told them they were done for the night. Johnny yelled to the crowd that the show would go on at his apartment and gave the address. Most of the crowd stayed behind, but Charles was among the dozen or so friends and followers who had come over that night for music, wine and smoke until the early morning.

Shirlee pushed the door to the apartment house open, stepped through and found Charles leaning against the five story stucco building, a character out of his own movie. His 6 foot skinny frame was dressed in stove pipe yellow pants, a red silk shirt and black ankle boots. He motioned to Shirlee, asking silently if she wanted a hit off his joint. When she declined, he crushed it out against the wall of the building and stuck what remained of the smoke in his shirt pocket.

"I'm going for a walk," said Shirlee, heading south on Van Nuys. "What's up?"

"I know you're gonna think this is strange, but I had to speak to you and Johnny," he said, falling in alongside Shirlee. "He has to be careful."

"What are you talking about, Charles?" Strange? Charles was always strange. And it wasn't only the way he dressed.

His emotional swings were all too evident, going from raving enthusiasm to abject depression, all in the same night sometimes. Shirlee suspected he was bipolar, something her mother back in Fresno had made her all too familiar with.

"Listen," continued Charles. "I had a dream. Johnny was in danger. Some hard looking dudes had cornered him and he was in real physical peril."

"It's a dream, Charles," said Shirlee dismissively.

"No, no. This was too real," insisted Charles. "This happens to me. When I dream something and it feels like this, it happens. Just last week I dreamed I was walking up the block in Tarzana and some guys in a car were yelling at me. In the dream they were about to grab me when I heard a loud bang. I was safe. And then I woke up."

"So? That was a dream."

"No. I mean, yeah. But two days later I was walking home and a carful of guys were yelling at me, making fun of my clothes. Two of them came out of the car and started to chase me. I ran as fast as I could, into my apartment and banged the door shut. Bang! Just like the dream!" Charles was wide-eyed and panicked, as if those guys were steps away from him now.

"Okay, Charles, okay. Calm down." Shirlee didn't believe the premonitions, but knew Charles believed them. "Do you remember anything else about your dream with Johnny? Who the other guys were or where they were?" They had reached the corner park where the only trees in the neighborhood stood and Shirlee took a deep breath of what she thought was the oxygen rich air.

"Humm," murmured Charles, thinking. "I don't know. Maybe they were Hispanic. Or maybe just dark skinned. I don't know. Sorry."

"That's okay." It was only a dream anyway. Charles is such a weirdo, Shirlee thought, dismissing the entire conversation. They continued their walk in the park.

CHAPTER 4

Johnny scanned the room, eyeing all the customers in the Bank of America branch on Wilshire Boulevard. In his uniform he looked much more able then the usual senior citizen employees who had these security guard jobs in most bank branches, but he often felt like a fraud. Not that he couldn't handle himself. The incident with Brick and Mr. Big had proven that. That and the .32 on his hip, on which he trained weekly at the firing range in Burbank.

But look at this place, he thought from his station by the front door. Mostly older customers, which to Johnny meant anyone over forty, waiting in orderly lines to deposit their cash or get some cash from the tellers who were lined up safely behind bulletproof see-through glass partitions. A few bank executives, sitting at desks on the floor, handling specific customer issues, opening accounts, filing loan applications. All about as exciting as a cup of warm milk. Who or what was he handling security for? It was all show. People expected an armed security guard/private cop at the bank, so that's what they got.

"Watson," a male voice called from behind him. It was Gene Murphy, Johnny's short, round, balding supervisor, in his 40's and with twenty years on the job. Johnny turned toward Murphy. "It's your break time. Fifteen minutes."

Johnny nodded in Murphy's direction and walked through a door into an employee break room. A small kitchen, refrigerator, microwave, sink, the usual apparatus. Johnny took a paper cup and poured a cup of coffee from a pot that had been brewed four hours before. The burnt smell wafted into his nostrils as he took the first harsh sip. His cell phone rang, playing the first four notes of The Beatles' "Here Comes The Sun."

"Hello?" he answered, not recognizing the number. "Who's this?"

"Johnny?" the male voice was barely audible, but sounded familiar. "That you? It's Rog."

"Rog! How are you, man? I didn't expect to hear from you. You were out of it the other day."

"Yeah, yeah. Listen, mate. I need you to come by the hospital," said Rog. "I gotta talk to you."

"Yeah. Okay, man. I can come by after work tomorrow…"

"No, mate. Today," said Rog, the urgency evident in his voice. "We need to speak today."

"Well," said Johnny, thinking he had to drop Shirlee at work after he got off at 4. "All right. I can probably get to the hospital around 5:30, maybe 6 depending on how bad traffic is. That okay?"

"Yeah, good. Thanks, mate. See you then." The phone line disconnected.

I wonder what this is all about, he thought, the anxiousness in Rog's voice raising unconscious alarms in his brain. He looked at his watch. Break time was almost up. He took one more gulp of the coffee, poured the remains into the sink, threw the cup into the trash and went back to his post by the door.

CHAPTER 5

"No, man. I haven't forgotten. I'll be there." Johnny couldn't believe it was Billy who was pestering him about making rehearsal on time. It was always the other way around. "No, no. I'll be done at the hospital and swing back out to the valley after. Should be there by 8. Call Frankie, make sure he knows. Okay, bye." Johnny pressed the disconnect button with one hand as he maneuvered his blue Honda Civic, old, battered but dependable, out of Laurel Canyon and through the streets of Hollywood.

Johnny knew Olivia, Billy's girlfriend and the band's drummer, would know about the rehearsal. He just was uncertain about Frankie, their teenage bass player. Since graduating high school, his natural popularity with girls had influenced him to try his hand at modeling and acting. Surprisingly, in a town where every good-looking kid in the country, or even the world, thinks they can show up and be the next Brad Pitt or Margot Robbie, Frankie was actually getting some work. He had appeared in some print ads for the Grove, an upscale outdoor mall next to the old Farmer's Market on Third Street, showing off copies of *L.A. Magazine* at the last gig, his oh so serious skinny pretty boy face staring sullenly at the camera. And he was working with an agent on getting auditions for TV spots and commercials. The kid was in demand. Which is why he needed Billy to make sure Frankie remembered about tonight. The band was playing at Slim's over on Lankershim in North Hollywood next week, trying out some new material and he wanted to get things as tight as possible beforehand. Hopefully traffic would let up enough by the time he left the hospital to get there on time.

Johnny turned right on Beverly Boulevard and followed the stop and go traffic until he saw the visitor parking signs for Cedars-Sinai Hospital on the right. He parked in the lot, taking a ticket on the way in, walked down the stairs to the entrance and retraced his steps from the other day to Rog's room. Johnny found Rog in an altogether different state today, wide awake, sitting up and impatiently flipping through TV channels with the bedside remote control.

"Bollocks," Rog complained to no one in particular. "A lot of rubbish. Talk shows, car chases and petty burglaries. Oh, hey, Johnny. There ya are. Come over here." He motioned Johnny in and to the side of the bed and clicked off the TV.

"Hey, Rog," said Johnny, looking him over. "How's it goin? Feelin better?"

"How's it goin?" said Rog. "Bloody look at me. Half my body's in a bloody cast. Doc says I won't be walking for weeks. Can't work. How'am I gonna earn, huh? Jesus."

"There's unemployment insurance, right?" Johnny said, trying to be encouraging.

"Pennies," said Rog, his left hand gesturing upward, waving off the suggestion. "I can't live off that. But that's what I wanted to talk to you about. Come here." He wagged his head, urging Johnny closer.

"You know, mate, between you and me, and you can't be spreadin this around," Rog said, "but my manager's pay at the club wasn't my sole source of income." He looked at Johnny with eyebrows raised, as if Johnny would understand.

Johnny had heard the rumors. Every music club had its sources. People who were always at the club with the recreational drugs of the moment. Whether it was pot, coke, e, acid, oxy, meth, speed, downers, junk, whatever, in whatever combination at any given time, there was always someone there to supply you with whatever would goose the night for you, supercharge the evening and galvanize that good time into bliss. And word was that Rog was the man at his place, the Whiskey, the most storied club in Los Angeles, even if it had fallen steeply from its glory days to its present, mostly pay-to-play, hard times.

"Well," said Johnny hesitantly, "I had heard that you were the one to see at the club if you needed anything." It made sense. Rog was always there. He knew all the regulars and rumor was that he did some time in a British jail before emigrating and landing in L.A.

"Yeah. Well," Rog said, motioning Johnny closer. He continued in a voice only slightly above a whisper. This conversation wasn't meant to be overheard by his roommate or a nurse stopping in. "You know, I had the place wired. Everyone knew that if they needed a taste, they'd speak to me or one of my guys. Like Big Tim. Your bud Billy knew. He bought weed from me more than once. I was bringing in some major coin every month."

Johnny shook his head, waiting for Rog to get to the point.

"So, I've been thinking," Rog continued. "This whole thing couldn't have been random. With me out of the picture, someone is going to be stepping in and taking advantage of the situation. There's too much money out there. And there are too many players around."

Johnny looked at Rog quizzically. Players. "What are you saying? That you were set up? The fight and you getting smashed up was planned?"

"That's it exactly!" replied Rog, slicing his left arm down in excitement.

"Well then, who…"

"Not sure. Could be anyone. There's enough rats in that sinkhole to cause a plague." Rog scratched his head and rubbed his week-old gray beard. "I want you to help me with this."

"Me?"

"Yeah. You could find out who's stepped into my shoes there. Who's managing the place and, more important, who's dealin now."

"I don't know, Rog. Won't people be suspicious?"

"Naw. You know people at the club and people know you. You're a familiar face, right? A local musician asking to buy drugs is as mundane as it gets."

"Yeah. And what if I do find out? Then what?"

"Let me know and I'll take it from there. Okay?"

"Shit, Rog. I wanna help you out and all. But this is all cloak and dagger stuff. Might be dangerous"

"Hell, kid. You can handle yourself, Mr. Security Guard. And I know you were involved in that Mr. Big craziness last year. I can pay, you know." Rog paused. "Listen, mate," he said, softening his tone. "Just find out the names for me. I promise it'll be worth your while."

Johnny exhaled audibly. He didn't like this. The thought that there was more here than Rog was saying came to mind. His eyes wandered out the window to the cars driving along

Beverly Boulevard, the cars outnumbering the pedestrians, and saw that the sky was turning dark, the sun having set. But he did owe the guy. Rog had booked his band Conflict to open for a name headliner or two, without making them pay for tickets, more than once. And he was managing the band, whatever that entailed for a struggling group.

"All right," Johnny finally said. "I'll see what I can find out. No promises."

"Great. Great, kid."

"And either way, you have to keep booking the band whenever you get back."

"Absolutely," agreed Rog. "And I can give you some cash too."

"Yeah, okay." Johnny looked at his watch. "I gotta go. Rehearsal tonight." He stood to leave.

"Right," said Rog, reaching for the remote control. "Let me know." He clicked on the TV. "And thanks, mate. The Mona Lisa!" He was already absorbed in an episode of *Jeopardy*.

"Sure. I'll see you soon."

Johnny left the room and exited the hospital. He retrieved his car, paid the $12 parking fee for a forty minute stay and raced down the street as fast as the Honda and traffic would let him. Thirty-five minutes to get to Van Nuys, he thought.

CHAPTER 6

Johnny could hear the rat-tat-tat of a snare drum being played and the deep twang of a bass guitar being tuned as he stepped through the heavy, thickly padded door. The band had begun practicing in a different rehearsal space a few months ago when the previous spot, a six room facility in North Hollywood, had increased their rates. Again. It had gotten too popular with not only up and coming bands, but major acts as well, so basic economics set in. The price of the rehearsal rooms went up and Conflict was out. Johnny and Billy spilt the cost of the rehearsal room and every dollar counted.

This room was one of three in Van Nuys that the owner housed in an industrial warehouse area off Sherman Way, a main alternate thoroughfare to the Ventura Freeway. Each of the rehearsal rooms was separated by storage garages and the entrance to each was through a single door. Johnny saw himself in the brownish tinged glass mirror covering the entire wall opposite where the amps and drums were set up. Handy for practicing their rock star poses. The room was twelve feet from the back wall to the mirror and twenty feet lengthwise. A tight little rectangle.

Olivia was the one rat-a-tatting behind the DW drums, striking each drum and then tightening or loosening the drum head with a drum key. She had a Bangles tee shirt on, slit at the neck, and lifted her head in greeting to Johnny.

Frankie was in his usual place in the corner, finishing his tuning and turning to the Ampeg bass amplifier behind him for a satisfying tone and volume. For once he didn't have a girl sitting nearby, staring in teenage sexual admiration. Johnny had to admit that he was a bit jealous of the kid's natural attractiveness, even if Johnny was over the moon in love with Shirlee.

"Hey, Frank," Johnny called out in greeting. "Girls finally had enough of you?" He walked toward the middle of the set-up, set down and opened his guitar case and plugged his Strat into a Fender Reverb amp to the right of the drums.

"Yeah, mahn," Billy answered for him from the other side of the drums, his Telecaster guitar slung low below his waist. He played a string of notes that blasted out of the speaker box sitting below a Marshall amp. "Poor Frankie only gets girls in photo shoots now. We'll have to put him on Tinder for company."

Frank looked up and a slight grin crossed his face. "Yeah. Thanks," he said quietly. "Not necessary."

Johnny laughed. "Okay, everyone good?" he asked, stepping to the microphone. Nods and "yeahs" all around. "Wha d'ya say we try "Holdin' On"?" Livie, count it off."

Olivia clicked her drum sticks together for five evenspaced beats at a moderate tempo, said "Two, three, four" and the band kicked in. Billy played a minor key blues run for two bars, everyone stopped for a beat and then jumped back in. Johnny sang.

"Look at us, we're all alone." Billy echoed the vocal with a stinging answer on guitar.

"No one here, they're all at home.

"Will we ever escape from here?

"Will I ever dry your tears?

"Who knows what tomorrow may bring, we've got to keep holding on.

"Who knows what tomorrow may bring, we've got to keep holding on."

Johnny stepped back from the microphone, echoed the melody of the last vocal phrase twice on guitar and stepped back to the mike.

"People come and people go." Billy added guitar.

"But this is something that I know.

"Without you, where would I be?

"Without your love, the world is empty.

"Who knows what tomorrow may bring, we've got to keep holding on.

"Who knows what tomorrow may bring, we've got to keep holding on."

Billy stepped up and played a soaring guitar solo, seemingly echoing the mournful, yet hopeful lyrics of the song. The band surged behind him, Frankie laying an undercurrent of bass notes, supporting the band, Olivia pounding away, the strength and power emanating from the drums belying her thin frame. Johnny strummed the chords of the tune, alternating a solid rhythm with ringing power chords. He stepped back to the mic and sang.

"Who knows what tomorrow may bring, we've got to keep holding on.

"Who knows what tomorrow may bring, we've got to keep holding on."

The entire band played the melodic phrase, played it again softer and one more time even quieter. They then all played it one last time at full volume and ended on a piercing high note and a thump on the drums. The band looked at each other, grins on their faces.

"Okay," said Johnny. "What's next on the hit parade?"

CHAPTER 7

Two hours later, Johnny was twisting his guitar cord and putting it into the case as everyone packed up. The time had passed in what seemed like moments to Johnny. Frankie had left first, claiming he had to get his beauty rest. Johnny figured he had someone waiting for him.

Billy and Olivia were in the corner of the room, talking seriously, Olivia's words' "…be kidding…" floated heatedly across the room. She turned and strode out the door, leaving Billy trailing behind in her angry wake.

"Hey, Billy," called Johnny. "Wait a sec." He grabbed his guitar case and hurried out the door, just as Olivia was driving away in the Subaru SUV, leaving Billy standing on the sidewalk.

"What was that all about?" asked Johnny.

"Nothing," Billy replied, although it was obvious to his friend by the pained look on Billy's face that that wasn't true.

"It'll be okay, man," said Johnny, trying to be consoling. "How many times have you and Livie been through this? You should be used to it."

"Yeah, s'pose so," said Billy, although he didn't look convinced. "Can you give me a ride home?"

"Sure, man. But I wanted to talk to you about something. Can you come with me to the Whiskey tonight?"

"Someone playin there?"

"Naw. I saw Rog earlier and he asked me to do him a favor. To stop by the club and see how things were going." He explained the substance of his talk with Rog earlier that evening. "I could use some backup. Not that I expect any real problems."

"Yeah," said Billy. "I'm for dat. Give Livie some coolin down time, not seein my blonde dredded ass for a few hours."

"Come on," said Johnny, walking toward his car and piling the guitar case in the back seat. "Let's go to my place, get something to eat. We can be at the club by 11."

They climbed in and Johnny started the car, pulling it onto Sherman Way, heading west.

"What was that all about with Livie?" Johnny asked as they bumped along the potholed street that was years past its due date for repairs.

"Oh, you know," said Billy. "Same ol' thing."

Johnny didn't know, but didn't want to press it. If Billy wanted to talk about it, he would.

CHAPTER 3

According to the marquee hanging over the corner of the club on Sunset and Holloway, tonight the acts featured and performing were "Charlotte Chartreuse," "The Pimp Daddies" and "Rock Star, Jr." Seems right for a Monday night, thought Johnny, as he and Billy approached the entrance. No name, probably pay-to-play acts, doing their best to get noticed and to put performing at the famous club on their social media.

"Hey, mahn," said Billy. "Which of dees people you tink are with which band? Dat couple dere…" pointing out two women in their twenties with the sides of their heads shaved and nose rings "…gotta be Chartreuse. And dos dere…" a group of five people their age, two African American men, one White man, and two women, one white, one black, "dos for Pimp Daddies. And dos there…" two couples in their forties, dressed in jeans, tee shirts and leather jackets "they mus'be here for their kiddies in Junior Rock Star. Wha ya tink?"

"I think for a rasta from the Valley," said Johnny. "You are one non-PC motherfucker." Billy's eyes got wide and he exploded with laughter. "Even if you might be right. Let's go in." They stepped toward the entrance of the club. Johnny had told Billy of his conversation with Rog on the ride into

Hollywood. The plan was to get to know the new manager and see if he or someone else was controlling things at the club. Things besides which bands were playing each night and which waitresses were working.

"Hey boys," said Tim, guarding the door. He put a hand the size of a catcher's glove on Johnny's shoulder. "You know everybody's gotta pay."

"Even us reg'lars?" asked Billy, feigned shock in his voice.

"Tim, Rog has been letting us in for a couple a weeks now," added Johnny, his eyes moving from Tim to the people milling about inside the entryway.

"I know, I know," said Tim, shaking his head. "But you know Rog ain't here. New management, new day, right? You know, it's only five dollahs. Right over at the window." He tilted his head to the side, indicating the side of the club where a young woman wearing horn rimmed glasses sat in a small booth behind a plexiglass window facing the street.

"Hey, Marge," said Johnny, reaching for his wallet. Marge had worked the ticket booth for as long as Johnny had been coming to the Whiskey. At least three years. Which for job longevity in music clubs, especially on the Sunset Strip, was forever. "Two please." He slid a ten dollar bill under the window. Marge picked it up with her thumb and forefinger, placed it in the cash drawer at her waist and placed two tickets under the window with her usual blank stare. Getting emotionally involved with customers, even regulars, was not her style.

"Good seein you too, Margie," said Billy, waving to her as he and Johnny went back to the entrance. They gave the tickets to Tim, who stamped their hands and ushered them into the club with a theatrical wave of his stanchion-sized arm.

Johnny stopped and put a hand on Tim's outstretched arm. "Hey, Tim," he said. "So who's running the place now that Rog is out? There a temporary manager?"

Tim looked at Johnny's hand on his arm and up at Johnny in warning. Johnny smiled at Tim and removed his hand.

"You know Les, right?" said Tim, turning his head to the next customer walking toward the entrance and dismissing Johnny. "Think he's upstairs."

Johnny and Billy entered the club and were assaulted by the music blasting from the speakers hanging from the walls. In the dim light Johnny could barely see a small knot of people standing below the stage on the dance floor. On the raised stage, a band consisting of three boy instrumentalists and one girl singer, all under the age of sixteen, playing a rock version of Katy Perry's song "Roar." The girl, who Johnny thought was probably still in junior high, was clutching the microphone and shaking her head, throwing out the vocals in a surprisingly strong voice. The band behind her, guitar, keyboards and drums, chugged along, transforming the empowerment anthem into a blues like romp.

"Not bad, huh" yelled Johnny into Billy's ear. Billy shook his head in response. They watched the kids play for a moment until Johnny motioned Billy to follow him. They passed the downstairs bar, where only a man and a woman were standing, nursing highballs and watching the show, and made their way up the stairs to the left of the stage. Walking behind the bench seats overlooking the stage, they headed toward the dressing rooms and office. The walls were thick with graffiti. Band and people's names, from famous like "Green Day" and "Van Halen" to unknown and probably one-time performers like "The Strutters" and "Willie Black," phone numbers, with and without come-ons, hundreds of drawings of everything from death heads to penises, various salutations, including "Rock Lives!", "Whiskey Rules!" and "Where's My Drink?!" and a thousand band stickers dating from the early days to the present, most faded and half torn, pasted one on top of the other, decorated the hallway. They came to a closed door, the same door Johnny had rushed through only a few days before on the night Rog was injured, and knocked.

"Wha is it?" Johnny heard from inside. "Hold up. One minute." They heard banging behind the door like furniture being rearranged or drawers being slammed closed. "All right, all right. Whaddya want?" Johnny opened the door and, with Billy alongside, stepped inside.

CHAPTER 3

"It's not the same," said Olivia, brushing her hair off her forehead and picking up the glass already half drained of Chardonnay. She took another healthy sip.

"It never is, is it?" Shirlee said, taking a drink from her own glass. They were sitting in the living room of the apartment that Shirlee and Johnny shared. The window shades were drawn and dim lamp lights and a few scattered candles combined to give a calming, yet eerie feeling, like the room of a trusted psychic on a rainy night. "And you and Billy have had plenty of ups and downs."

"But it's been so good in the last year. Ever since that horrible business with Harry went down and all that, me and Billy have been so in synch. He was even excited for me to join the band." She put the glass on the glass coffee table placed in front of the brown fabric couch on which they sat.

"The band has never sounded better," Shirlee encouraged her, pouring a refill into Olivia's glass and lighting a joint. Shirlee had gotten a call from Olivia minutes after the guys had headed into Hollywood, asking if she could come over. She arrived ten minutes later. She was upset, clutching Shirlee as she opened the door, her eyeliner smudged from crying. It wasn't as if Shirlee hadn't seen the signs in the past few weeks. Curt conversations, dismissive looks, each attending shows, dinners and parties without the other. It was obvious that Olivia and Billy were having some problems.

"Yeah, I'm really loving playing, ya know," Olivia continued. "But he doesn't understand that I need more. Why else would I have put myself through that paralegal program at UCLA? And this is a good job offer. I bet it pays more than what any of the four of us are making now. Can you imagine working at a movie studio?" She kicked her shoes off, took the offered joint from Shirlee and took a deep drag.

"Sounds fantastic," said Shirlee, brushing some ash off her lap. "Why does he say he doesn't want to move?"

"Says it's his mother. Doesn't want to be too far from the nursing home for his weekly visits. Then we can't afford it. Then he doesn't even wanna talk about it. I don't know what his problem is." She paused and took a gulp of wine. "Hollywood is not that far. But I don't want to fight traffic every day into Paramount. And you should see the apartment. It's really nice. Two bedrooms, a quiet street off Larchmont. I could walk to work. Oh hell." Olivia pulled the red wool sweater she was wearing over her head as she sprawled out on the couch, her feet on Shirlee's lap.

"You know, maybe something else is bothering him," said Shirlee, stroking Olivia's feet. "He hasn't been very happy at that job at Active."

"Yeah, who would be?" Oliva said. "You and Johnny don't have this problem, do you? I just don't know what he's thinking anymore. The only thing I know that's important to him is the band. At least we have that in common." Her voice got quieter as she spoke, her eyes closed, the teetering wine glass rescued by Shirlee, who placed it on the table.

"Why don't you sleep here tonight?" suggested Shirlee. She eased out from under Olivia's legs, placed the Indian-patterned blanket draped over the couch on her, blew out the candles and switched off the lamps.

Her phone rang. Shirlee recognized the number.

"Charles?" she answered, walking quickly into the bedroom so as not disturb Olivia. "Why're you callin so late?"

"Shirlee, sorry," said Charles, urgency in his voice. "I don't have Johnny's number, so I called you. I just had another dream. You gotta warn Johnny!"

"What are you talking about, Charles? You sound hysterical."

"A bunch of guys surrounded him and then he disappeared! Vanished! You gotta warn him!"

"Charles. Calm down. It was a dream. Take a deep breath, smoke a joint and go back to sleep."

"But…"

"Good night, Charles." Shirlee disconnected. First Olivia and then Charles, she thought. A night full of traumas. Maybe it's a full moon.

She stripped off her jeans and laid down under the covers on the bed. She stared out the window at the streetlight, a hazy yellow against the night sky. After a few minutes she was asleep.

CHAPTER 10

The room looked the same to Johnny as it did four days before. Same big desk on one side of the room, chairs scattered throughout. Posters of famous alumni Jim Morrison and Eddie Van Halen on the walls. A different girl hovering behind the desk, but she might've been that other girl's twin sister. Too young to be here and wiping white powder from her nose. Johnny could hear the muted sounds of Rock Star Jr. ending their last song, a crescendo of music flooding up from downstairs and from behind the wall length glass partition at the far end of the office.

"Who are you?" asked the man seated behind the desk. He had curly brown hair piled high on top of his head and shaved sides. A thin face and prominent nose, he wore a black suit jacket and a white shirt. Johnny recognized Les as one of Rog's security guys/go-fors, who he'd seen backstage hustling the bands onto the stage and hanging out by the back door in the alleyway. A tall, thin guy, Johnny always thought he talked with more authority than he had, punching above his weight class.

"Hey," said Johnny. "You know me. Johnny from the band "Conflict"? And you know Billy."

"Ya mahn," Billy chimed in. "How's it be?"

"Yeah, okay," said Les, pulling a drawer open and taking out a vial of white powder. He dug a spoon into the vial, placed it by his nose and inhaled, the powder vacuumed up. "So whaddya want?"

"Well," Johnny started. "Are you the manager now that Rog is out? Cause we had been talking to him about another gig soon. You know, nothing was decided, but we thought, maybe if you're the new manager we could set something up. Ya know?" They hadn't spoken much in the past and Johnny thought it best to play the spaced out musician at least until he knew this guy better.

"I don't know," said Les. "We might be goin in a new direction. Maybe D.J.'s. You like to dance, don't ya, darling?" he asked the young girl. She smiled and shook her head.

"Naw," said Billy. "D.J.'s? This the Whiskey, man, not some disco bottle club."

"Is this your decision?" asked Johnny. "Are you the new manager?"

"Yeah, I'm the fuckin manager," insisted Les, abruptly standing. "And if I want to charge $300 for a bottle of wine and clear that useless stage out of here, I will. Fuckin' musicians."

"Hey man," said Johnny. "We're just looking for a gig, all right? Whaddya say?" He saw Les' eyes jerk toward the door as it swung open and three men walked in, all big, long haired and wearing jean jackets. Johnny wasn't sure but they might've been the bikers who had smashed up Rog the other night.

"Yeah, all right," said Les, suddenly eager for the conversation to end. "I'll think about it. Come back in a few days, okay?"

"Sure, mahn," said Billy. "We see ya soon." He and Johnny edged past the bikers and walked toward the door. The bikers ignored them, went right to the desk and standing, surrounded Les. Johnny noticed the logo on the back of their jackets. It read "Death Playas."

Johnny and Billy left the office and the young girl ducked out as the door was being closed. She smiled thinly at them and walked down the hall. Johnny and Billy exchanged glances.

"Whacha tink?" asked Billy. "Dat guy sure was squirrely."

"Yeah," agreed Johnny. "And it looked like he was about to have a very uncomfortable meeting. Let's split up and try to cop. See who's doin what now that Rog is gone. You speak to Vibes at the bar. I'll circulate. Find out what you can. Have some money?"

"Yeah, all good," replied Billy, patting his shirt pocket. "Meet up in half hour out front."

They headed down the stairs to the rock/rap sounds of the Pimp Daddies. Billy walked to the bar opposite the stage as Johnny faded from sight in the darkness of the club. No one was left at the bar except for a broad shouldered black guy in a white tee shirt and jeans, a yellow bandana on his head. He was wiping the bar with a damp, dirty towel and looked up as Billy approached.

"Bates, man, the white rasta," he said, smiling at Billy and his blond dreadlocks. Vibes offered a fist clasp and they shook. "How ya been? Drink?"

"Is good, Vibes. Tanks. I have me a beer. Wha'ever ya got."

"Okay. No Red Stripe though." Vibes laughed and reached under the counter, coming up with a wet bottle of Budweiser. "Glass?" he asked.

"Naw," replied Billy. Vibes wiped the water and ice off the bottle, opened it and placed it on the bar.

Billy had met Vibes the first time he had come to the club a couple of years ago. A good natured, talkative guy in his mid-thirties who seemed to get along with everyone, he could also mix a drink as needed. A perfect bartender. Rumor had it that he had been in combat in Afghanistan and the tattoo on his arm of a green bomb hurtling through the air with the words "Bombs Away" emblazoned on it did nothing to dispel that rumor.

Billy took a swig of the Bud.

"Hey, mahn," Billy said, looking over his shoulder at the stage where one of the Pimp Daddies was furiously rapping to a hard rock rhythm. "How are tings round here, now? Is Les de man now?"

"Weellll…," said Vibes drawing the word out cautiously. "If you ask him he is. But it's a little hard to believe. Such a weak cunt." He looked past Billy, scanning the crowd. "Marv, the owner, came by Saturday before opening to say Les is acting manager, but I doubt he's calling the shots. Wha the…"

Billy turned, following Vibes' line of vision. Big Tim was racing through the crowd, heading for the back of the club. Billy followed, pushing past gawking friends of the band. He exited through the back door into the alleyway between the club and the parking lot.

"Break it up, you assholes," hollered Tim, as he reached down to the two figures grappling on the asphalt ground, rolling, arms swinging wildly, legs kicking. Tim pulled off the guy on top and Billy saw it was Johnny. The other guy, a young Hispanic, a bantamweight around 5' 5", jumped up and tried to get at Johnny, but was stopped by Tim's outstretched arm. "Easy, Pancho," warned Tim. The Hispanic guy's eyes flared, but he stopped dead in his tracks when he saw how huge Tim was.

"What the hell's goin on?" Les had come down from the office, the three bikers standing behind him.

"Nothin, boss," said Tim. "I got this. Right?" asking Johnny and the other combatant. They both grudgingly nodded.

"All right," said Les. "Go the fuck home." He turned and went back inside. The bikers stayed.

"What happened, man?" said Billy as he pulled Johnny away from the crowd.

"Nothin," said Johnny. "I was trying to score some E. This guy said he had the hook up, then grabbed my money and tried to take off." He showed Billy the crumpled dollars in his hand. "Didn't get far."

"You, okay?" said Tim, coming over after telling the Hispanic guy to take off. "You should've come to me, man. Jus cause Rog is gone, doesn't mean I'm out of the loop."

"You're dealin?" asked Billy.

"Tsk, no," said Tim, amused at the ridiculousness of the question. "But see those dudes there?" He pointed to the bikers, none of whom had moved back inside. "They have whatever you want. Okay?" He patted some dirt off Johnny's back and looked at his cheek. "Get that cut looked after." He turned and walked back into the club.

"Whaddya think?" Billy asked. "Should we ask them for something?"

No," said Johnny. "It's late. We both have work tomorrow. Let's get out of here. I'll let Rog know what we found out." They walked by the bikers as they left the alley, who gave them the once over but didn't say a word. They turned the corner toward Sunset, found Johnny's car and headed back to the Valley.

CHAPTER 11

Rog was sitting up in bed the following evening when Johnny came into the hospital room. The other bed was empty and an orderly was cleaning that side of the room, throwing out used plastic cups, changing the sheets.

"Give me a hand, would'ja, mate." Rog swung his legs over the side of the bed, taking the heavy cast in his hands and putting it on the floor. "Cut yourself shaving?" noticing the bandage on Johnny's cheek. "Bring that over here," he said, indicating the wheelchair. "I gotta get me some air."

Johnny, still in his security guard uniform having come straight from work, swung the chair around and placed the seat by the bed. He reached under Rog's shoulders, lifted him off the bed and lowered him onto the wheelchair.

"Man, that cast adds twenty pounds," said Johnny, breathing heavily. "And you're no lightweight to begin with."

"Well, your gun put a crease in my side, Officer Whoops," said Rog, lifting his hospital gown and showing Johnny a red mark on his hip. "Let's get goin."

Johnny grabbed the handles and pushed Rog out of the room and down the hallway. Three women in nurses uniforms paused only briefly from their paperwork as they went by, the sight of a young, long haired security guard in fully armed uniform pushing a heavy set half naked gray haired guy with a full leg cast apparently not such an unusual occurrence for them.

Down the hall they went, Johnny dutifully pushing while Rog gave a running commentary.

"Now see here," he said, pointing at a room on the right. "I hear that the dudes in there had pneumonia. Nurses were right nervous about them when they first came in from the emergency room. Ventilators at the ready. And over there…" pointing ahead "that there's the ICU. Best to stay clear of that place. Sick when you go in, sicker afterwards, I bet. Ah, here we go. Down, mate, down to the blessed ground."

Johnny pressed the elevator button and the doors opened after a minute. An Hispanic nurse, 5" 3", brown hair tied behind the white nurses cap, with a name tag that read "Torrez" pinned above her breast, stepped out.

"Mr. Cray," she said, looking at Rog. "Where are we going?"

"Ah, good day, Nurse Torrez," replied Rog. "We're not goin anywhere. But me and my friend Johnny here are going downstairs for some fresh air."

"Now you know the doctor said to stay in bed for another two days." Torrez gave him her best stern schoolmarm squint.

"It'll be a little secret between us, darlin. Right?"

Torrez smiled "All right, Mr. Cray. Ten minutes and get your butt back up here. Right?"

"You're the boss," said Rog, giving her a wink. "Ah damn, now we lost the elevator."

Five minutes later Johnny and Rog were sitting outside the entrance to the hospital, side by side, Rog in the wheelchair, Johnny on a concrete bench. The sun was setting and the fading blue sky was turning orange in the distance.

Johnny relayed what had happened at the club the night before, talking with Les, Billy's conversation with Vibes, the incident in the alley and the presence of the Death Playas bikers, who, according to Tim, had taken over the drug concession.

"Death Playas," said Johnny. "You said 'Players' the first night you were in here."

"I did?" Rog looked skeptical. "I don't recall." He stared at the traffic on the street, thinking. "But you know, doesn't surprise me. I knew Les was friendly with those guys. Think he has a brother who's a biker. Maybe one of them." He watched the traffic some more and then looked at Johnny, an idea forming.

"What?" demanded Johnny. "I don't like that look."

"It's nothing, mate, nothing," insisted Rog. "I just need someone to scope out the Playas. Maybe pay them a little visit."

"Rog, you said get you the names and you'd handle it. I got you names."

"I know, I know. But I have to find out who's calling the shots. Is it Les? Someone with the Playas? That would surprise me. The word was always that they didn't have a decent connection. That's why they were never a threat. Why now?"

"Listen, man," said Johnny, exasperated that his good deed was mushrooming out of control. "I did you a favor. I'm not into getting in the middle of a drug war."

"Yeah, I understand," said Rog, seemingly backing off. Then he reversed again. "But, how's this. I'll give you a thousand for what you've already did. And another two grand if you go to the Playas bar north of Pass and get some more intel."

"They won't tell me anything. I'm an outsider."

"They have bands playing there sometime. You could say you're lookin for a gig. Come on, man. If I'm out, I'm done. I'll be standing on line at the unemployment office. Make it another five grand."

Five grand, Johnny thought. More than I brought home in two months.

"All right," he said finally. "But next time I see you ya better have the money for me."

"Absolutely. Guaranteed. Now let's go back in. My ass is getting cold."

What have I got myself into, thought Johnny, as he wheeled Rog back into the hospital, up the elevator and back into his room.

"Have a nice time, Mr. Cray?" said Nurse Torrez, entering the room and helping Rog back into bed.

"I'll see you later," said Johnny, turning to leave.

"The Hungry One," called out Rog. "The bar's called the Hungry One."

CHAPTER 12

It starts with a sound. A buzzing in my head like a fly on a lazy summer night that won't leave me be. That hovers, dives in and circles me and then flits away before I can catch it, swat it, shoo it away. Or a sound like a scrapping of car fenders against the wall, I cut that turn too tight. Or the bumping, clanging of the train as it hurtles over the tracks, the rhythmic cadence that reminds me of that phrase my father/mother/uncle/aunt always said in just that rhythm, that number of syllables. With a melodic variation that catches me by surprise but sounds perfectly natural, as if it's been here the entire time. The rise and fall of the traffic on the street, on the freeway, interspersed with the honking of horns and the yelling of irate drivers.

No, wait. It starts with a word, a phrase. A remark tossed off by the TV newscaster, by the grocery clerk as he bagged the food, my neighbor who's talking to his dog. In any other instance it sounds like nothing. Nothing extraordinary. Run of the mill spoken language. But today it's heightened, elevated, unique enough to stand out and imprint itself into my head like a signpost in the middle of the desert.

And I'll run down that road, singing that phrase in that rhythmic, melodic buzz until it tumbles out of lips and out of my hands and out into the world, forming and then fully formed. Recognize it? It's so familiar but so brand new. Name that tune.

CHAPTER 13

It was close to midnight when Johnny returned from the hospital and opened the door to his apartment.

He could make out the sleeping figure on the couch in the dim light seeping in from the street. Her blond hair splayed across the cushion under her head, it was definitely Olivia. He walked as quietly as his Doc Marten crepe soled security guard shoes would allow, squeaking in the night-time silence on the worn fake wood flooring leading into the bedroom.

"That you, baby?" Shirlee's tired voice, only slightly above a whisper, rose up from the bed.

"Yeah, it's me," answered Johnny, reaching his hands out to find the bed. He sat and undressed. "Shove over." He turned down the blanket, slid in and replaced the blanket on top of them both, draping his arm across Shirlee's shoulder. Shirlee wiggled into him.

Baby," Johnny whispered into her ear. "How long is Livie gonna be here? You know she's welcome, but this can't be a permanent situation. She's drivin Billy nuts."

Shirlee softly giggled. "Drivin Billy Bates bats," she said. No laughter from Johnny. "Okay. Okay, baby. I'll speak to her about it tomorrow. Maybe one more night, all right?"

"Yeah, okay," replied Johnny. He reached over her shoulder, cupped her small perfect breast and nuzzled her neck.

"Hmm, that's nice, baby," murmured Shirlee. "But I have an early shift tomorrow. Need my beauty rest or those pancakes won't get served."

"I'll help you sleep," said Johnny.

"Well, in that case…"

The next morning, Shirlee woke at 6 and left at 6:30 for her 7 a.m. shift at Norm's. Johnny laid in bed for another hour, shutting off the alarm on his iPhone right before it went off at 7:30. He showered, dressed again in his guard uniform and went into the kitchen area. He passed Olivia who was sitting up on the couch, rubbing the sleep from her eyes and stretching. She was wearing his Dodgers tee as a night shirt.

"Coffee?" he asked, raising the jar of Folgers instant.

"Uhmm, hum," she answered affirmatively. Olivia stood and padded into the small kitchenette, getting two mugs out of the cabinet and placing them on the counter. Johnny spooned in a scoop of coffee crystals into each and waited for the water to boil in the kettle.

"Sleep well?" asked Johnny, feeling awkward, waking up again to breakfast with his best friend's girl. He poured the water into the mugs.

"Good," said Olivia. "You know, Johnny, you and Shirl are so good together." She blew on the coffee and took a hesitant sip. "I just wish that me and Billy were so in synch."

"Wha d'ya mean? You and Billy have been together for years now. You may have your ups and downs, but you always get back stronger than ever." Johnny wondered as he said it whether he believed it or simply wanted to encourage Olivia to give Billy another chance. Or if he really just wanted to reclaim his apartment.

"Maybe," said Olivia. She had met Billy years before when Billy and Johnny had played as a duo in an area-wide high school talent contest. Held in Notre Dame High School's auditorium in Sherman Oaks, the best talent from all the San Fernando Valley high schools came for a one night showcase. Olivia was there as part of the All Valley award winning glee club. She could carry a tune for as long as she could remember and, with all the lessons she took, had envisioned herself at one time as an L.A. Alicia Keys until she burnt out on piano. That night, watching the show after she and the glee club had finished their a cappella performance of Gwen Stefani's "Hollaback Girl," she was captivated by this duo of two guitarists playing and sharing vocals on Green Day's "Time of Your Life." Especially the guy in dreads, whose funky appearance belied his wonderful playing and soulful singing. He was surprisingly shy when she told him later how much she enjoyed his performance. Their conversation and flirtation had continued until Johnny had interrupted them, saying he had to get home, his mother would be pissed if he was late. Olivia and Billy said goodbye and she pulled him in for a kiss. They'd been together, on and off, ever since.

Olivia took her mug into the living room, placed it on the coffee table, her back to Johnny, stripped off the tee shirt and slipped on a pair of jeans and a red tee shirt that had been discarded on the floor. Johnny tried to avert his eyes and not stare. She was a gorgeous girl.

"Er, I gotta go," said Johnny, putting his mug in the sink and fishing his car keys out from his jacket pocket. "Day after tomorrow is Slim's, right?" referencing the band's upcoming show. "You see Shirl later, tell her I won't be too late tonight." He walked to the door, carrying a gym bag. "See ya."

"Bye, Johnny," Olivia said, watching him shut the door behind him. Must be going to the gym later, she thought.

Johnny climbed into the Honda, started the engine and spun the steering wheel, pushing the car into traffic, heading for Beverly Hills. With his right hand he speed dialed Billy's number.

"Hey, Bill," he said when Billy answered on the third ring. "Can you meet me tonight at six-thirty in the Ralph's parking lot on Coldwater and Ventura? We gotta go to Pasadena… I'll tell you later…Yeah, she's still here…I know…See you then." He pressed the off button, swerved around a blue Tesla stopped in the middle of the street for no apparent reason and made a left onto the freeway on-ramp.

CHAPTER 14

"And we goin to some biker bar why now?"

Johnny paused before answering Billy's question. He had put in another full but typically uneventful day at the bank, the only thing breaking up standing at his post by the door being the occasional "Hello" or "Good Morning" from entering patrons. By afternoon the greetings, as usual, stopped, people getting on with their business, looking forward to the end of the workday.

Johnny had been looking forward to it as well. At least the end of his shift. The visit to The Hungry One, with some trepidation. He kept thinking of his conversation with Rog and how exactly he was going to approach this. Walk into a biker bar where he knew no one and be cool and casual? Asking about a gig was Rog's suggestion. As good a plan as any, although how that was going to lead to information about their drug dealing was completely unclear to him. I guess we'll have to improvise, thought Johnny. Like a cool jam session that starts out with the hint of a musical phrase and takes off from there. Considering that, he was glad Billy was joining. Strength in numbers. Plus after years of friendship and playing together, they knew each other's moves.

He had changed in the bank's employee bathroom into jeans, a Foo Fighters tee shirt, a worn blue baseball jacket and a pair of dirty white Chuck Taylor Converse sneakers, which had all been crumbled in a heap inside the gym bag he had brought from home. The security guard uniform went onto a hanger and deposited with his shoes into the trunk of the Honda. The .32 went into the back of his pants belt, just in case. Then he drove up Beverly Drive, past the Beverly Hills Hotel, into Coldwater Canyon, up and over the top of the Santa Monica mountains at Mulholland Drive and around and down into the valley. Traffic crawled, but Johnny was used to that. Trying to avoid L.A. traffic was a fool's game, Google Maps, Waze, whatever.

Pulling into the grocery store parking lot, Billy was waiting beside the Subaru SUV, smoking a joint and watching the customers filing in and out of the store, empty bags in their hands going in, bags full of groceries going out. Johnny pulled up alongside him, told Billy they'd pick up the Subaru later and pulled back into the street, heading for the 101 going east toward Pasadena.

Along the way Johnny told Billy where they were headed and the plan, such as it was, which even to Johnny's mind still wasn't much. He tried to explain it again to Billy.

"Look," he said, transitioning to the 134 freeway. "We talk to some of the guys there, ask about playing and casually ask about getting some dope. Pot or pills, nothing major. But only after we're there for a while and only if we're feeling okay about it. Any issues, any wobbly shit, we're out of there."

"Mahn, you must really be needin the dough ray me, brudda. You gonna share?"

"I'll split it with you. Okay?" Billy grunted his acceptance. "All right...Hey, I gotta ask you, what's up with you and Livie?"

"Oh, I don know, mahn. She buggin."

"Come on, Billy. You can't just brush this off. The girl's really upset. She told Shirlee you're balking at moving into Hollywood. What's the big deal?"

"What? Naw mahn, I tain't dat. Aw shit." Billy's face was strained, his cheeks pinched, his eyes clouded over. "Man, we had a fight, okay?" He crossed his arms and stared out the passenger side window, evading the discussion. But Johnny wasn't having it.

"So you had a fight. So what?" asked Johnny. "Get it together and tell her you're sorry. Done deal."

"I did that," insisted Billy. "You don get it." Billy took a deep breath. "She thought she was pregnant and I didn't react well. Fuck. I panicked and went wide-eyed. Asked her if she was gonna keep it. Shit. Turns out the test was negative, but the damage was done. I don even know why I said that. I love her and I could see us together and having kids. Took me by surprise, ya know?"

"Man, now I get it. No wonder Olivia's been sleeping on my couch all week." The 134 freeway merged into the 210 and Johnny looked for the Lake Avenue exit. "Hey, listen. You guys have been through worse. Remember when you couldn't keep your hands off that Giselle a couple of years ago? Not that I could blame ya."

"Yeah. But oh did Livie lemme ave it. 'member? The cops hadda break it up. Thought she was gonna kill me." Billy smiled at the memory. Olivia pummeling him with her fist in the street outside of a club in Santa Monica after seeing Billy and Giselle, a statuesque black girl who had come with Olivia to the gig, together in the back of the club, his hand on her ass, her hand down his pants. "That was the end of their friendship and almost the end of ours."

"Yeah. But it wasn't. You guys got past it. You'll get through this too."

"Maybe."

"You'll see." The exit sign announcing "Lake Ave." came up on the right. Johnny maneuvered the car around traffic and down the exit ramp. He made a left onto the boulevard and headed toward the hills above Pasadena.

CHAPTER 15

The densely populated streets of Pasadena led north into the suburban town of Altadena. A small civic center on Lake Street quickly faded as Johnny drove past the single family homes in the foothills of the San Gabriel Mountains. He turned left on East Loma Alta Drive for a half mile, until he came to a lone roadhouse with a flickering neon sign that proclaimed "The Hungry One," except the "T" in the first word and the "e" in the last were out, the sign actually reading "he Hungry On" in the dark.

Johnny parked the car in the dirt parking lot to the right of the wooden building, alongside dusty Ford pickups and a '90s Mustang. He and Billy exited and walked around the front, passing a row of 15 Harley Davidson motorcycles lining the road outside the bar, tricked out to the riders' personal tastes. High handle bars, chrome reflecting the neon and lone streetlight, mud flaps with silhouettes of voluptuous naked women, helmets left on the seats. "Iron Man" by Black Sabbath blasted out of two speakers hanging over the doorway as they walked up the steps and opened the door to the club.

The driving, dense music was twice as loud inside. It was dark and all Johnny could see at first were neon signs for Rolling Rock and Pabst over the bar along the right hand wall. They stood for a moment as their eyes adjusted to the gloom. Once they did, Johnny realized that every other eye in the place was focused on them. They froze for a moment, surveying the room. To their left along the far wall, half a dozen men with long hair, shoulder length, ponytailed, wearing jeans and black leather jackets stood around a pool table, two of them holding cues. To the right of them was a dusty, paint chipped Wurlitzer jukebox, which stood alongside a small wooden stage raised a foot off the linoleum floor and big enough for one person. Maybe they had comedians, thought Johnny. Or guest lecturers.

Between Billy and Johnny were a dozen tables, some empty, some crowded with men in the same jeans and leather and scattered women dressed the same.

In the time it took for Johnny to survey the club, every person took them in, dismissed them as either inconsequential or harmless or both and turned away, going back to their conversations, pool game and booze. Johnny nodded to Billy and they walked to the bar, wedging in beside a burly guy with the words "Death Playas" stitched into the back of his jeans jacket and a guy who could have been his brother except the words were tattooed on his bicep, drawn to look like they were dripping blood. The tattooed guy gazed at Billy.

"Nice tats, mahn," said Billy, nodding approvingly. The biker looked away.

"A couple of PBRs," requested Johnny from the round faced bartender, an easy two fifty, shaved head, a black stripe tattoo running up the left side of his neck, wearing a white apron splashed with beer.

One eye of the bartender moved in its socket to look at Johnny. The other eye didn't move. Glass, thought Johnny.

"No PBRs," the bartender said, hands on his hips.

Johnny looked at the guy sitting next to him, taking a long pull on a bottle of Pabst.

"All out?" Johnny asked.

"That's right. My man here had the last one."

"Okay then," said Johnny, eyeing bottles of beer in an ice filled sink on the other side of the bar. "Two of those Rollin Rocks."

"You have I.D.? I don't think you're old enough to drink."

"Come on, mahn," interjected Billy. He flipped open his wallet and showed the bartender his California drivers license. Johnny put his license on the bar.

"25? And you're 26?" The bartender shook his head. "I think you're high school kids and these are fakes."

The biker next to Johnny with the "Death Playas" jacket started laughing, a high coughing machine gun of a laugh. "Aw, give the kids a fuckin beer, Marty," he said. "Geez. You gotta break their balls."

Marty looked disgruntled, but popped the cap off a couple of Rolling Rock bottles and set them down on the bar with an audible clank. "Five dollars," he said. Johnny paid and Marty took the money and walked to the other end of the bar.

Johnny took a slug from the bottle. "Thanks, man," he said to the guy who had helped them out. "I'm Johnny." He offered his hand. The guy shook it, his huge fist engulfing Johnny's.

"Del," he said. "Tell me, Johnny. What the hell are you and your blond boyfriend doin here? I sure as shit never seen you before." The tone was pleasant and calm, contrasting with the threat evident in the words.

Johnny smiled. "No, he's not my boyfriend. He's in my

band. A helluva guitarist, really. You know, that's why we're here. We heard that you sometimes have bands playing here and we're looking for gigs."

"Really?" said Del. "You got a band? And you wanna play here?"

Before he could answer, Billy elbowed Johnny in the ribs.

"What? What is it, man?" asked Johnny, turning toward his friend.

"Look over there, by the pool tables," said Billy. "Aren't those the guys from the Whiskey the other night?"

Johnny turned to look. "How can you tell?"

"I'm sure of it. One of ems wearing the same giant belt buckle. 'Colt 45' with crossing pistols."

"You know Smokey?" said Del, overhearing the conversation. "From where?"

"Er, at the Whiskey," said Johnny.

"Yeah," said Billy. "He was hanging with Les, you know, the manager, in his office. Hey, do you think we could get some oxy?"

Johnny was alarmed, thinking Billy had overplayed his hand. But Del simply smiled.

"Sure, kid. Whatever ya need. Hey, Smokey," Del called out. "Come here." He waved Smokey over, who lumbered up to the bar. "These boys need some oxy. Why don't you take them in the office and set em up?"

Billy jumped off the stool. "I'll take care of it. Lead the way," he said to Smokey. Smokey looked at Del, who shook his head. They walked toward a door to the side of the small stage.

"So," said Del to Johnny, who lifted the beer to his lips. "How'd you know to come here for oxy?"

"We, er, we didn't," said Johnny hesitantly. "Billy probably thought that bikers…" he stopped when he saw Billy and Smokey go through the door, followed by the other two guys from the club. Johnny stood and Del pushed down on his shoulder, forcing him back onto the stool.

"Sit down," Del said, an order, not a suggestion.

Johnny acted instinctively, the lessons from his training kicking in. He went with the flow of Del's push, squatted down and forced Del off balance. Johnny pushed away from Del, knocking him off his stool and crashing to the floor. Johnny leaped up and raced to the door.

He could hear yelling from the other side as he reached for the doorknob. He jerked open the door and rushed in, Del and two other guys following behind him.

Billy was being held by one of the bikers as Smokey delivered a sweeping backhand blow to his face. Billy sagged in the biker's arms, blood erupting from his nose.

"Stop. Right now!" yelled Johnny. One of the bikers with Del ran up to Johnny, winding up to land a roundhouse punch. Johnny saw him out of the corner of his eye, ducked and evaded the punch and chopped down on the side of the biker's neck with both fists. The biker sprawled onto the floor.

Before another biker could get close to him, Johnny took the .32 out of his belt and fired a shot into the ceiling. "Bam!" Everybody froze.

Johnny turned and held the gun aimed at Del. "We're leaving now," he said. "Can you walk?" he asked Billy, who shook loose from the biker's grasp. Billy audibly inhaled through his nose and spat blood.

"Yeah," Billy said. "Let's get outta this pit."

Johnny kept the gun trained on Del as they backed out through the bar and out the door. A crowd followed him.

"Stay in there," shouted Johnny, halting their exit from the bar with a sweep of his gun arm. Billy reached the car first and flung the driver's door open for Johnny, who hopped in, started the ignition and stamped on the gas, sending dirt flying into the air.

Billy looked out the rear window of the car and could see Del slapping a hand on Smokey's chest, stopping him as he moved to go down the steps toward his bike. Billy could feel Del's eyes on him as they raced away.

CHAPTER 16

"Man," said Johnny heatedly, gripping the wheel as they sped down Lake Avenue toward the freeway. "What the fuck?! We were gonna scout it out, get in good with them and only then get into their drug business. Not act like a couple of 12 year olds outside the schoolyard."

Billy wiped his nose with his shirt sleeve and looked at the slight trickle of blood on his shirt. "I know, I know," he said. "I thought you were getting in with that Del asshole."

"Getting in?" questioned Johnny. "We hadn't been speaking for ten minutes. We'll never get anything out of them now."

"Yeah, guess so." Billy paused, looked out the side window with a smile on his face. "There goes a shot at a gig there."

Johnny looked at Billy like he was from another planet and then burst out laughing. Billy joined in.

"You are one crazy mofo," said Johnny, taking a deep breath and easing his grip on the steering wheel. "You okay? Need to go to the hospital?"

"No, it's nothing. Little nose bleed. Did you eat tonight? I'm starvin."

Twenty minutes later, they were sitting at the counter at Pie 'n Burger, a Pasadena culinary landmark since 1963, finishing off their burgers and waiting for their pies. They had arrived five minutes before closing. But the middle-aged waitress with a nametag that read "Emily" took one look at the bedraggled duo and took pity on them.

Emily placed the pies in front of them, cherry for Johnny, Dutch apple for Billy, put the check face down between them, smiled and said, "Take your time, boys."

"So wha next?" asked Billy, spooning a forkful of pie into his mouth. "Whacha gonna tell Rog?"

"Hell, I'm gonna tell him that you got your ass kicked and we were lucky to get out of there in one piece." He wondered if Rog would give him the money he promised even though he hadn't gotten any information about the drug trade at the club. And even if he got the information, how was Rog going to get back into the club and retake that "concession?" Well, it wasn't really his problem.

"Come on, man. Finish up." The restaurant was empty except for Emily, who was waiting by the cash register at the end of the counter.

Billy scraped the last of the crumble off his plate, wiped his mouth, stood and stretched. "That was good," he said.

Johnny gave Emily his credit card, added 20% to the total, signed the slip of paper and exited the restaurant, Billy alongside.

"You think Livie will be home tonight?" asked Billy. They drove down the street back toward the freeway, heading back to Billy's Subaru in the Ralph's parking lot.

"Don't know. Maybe. You gonna patch it up or what?"

Billy shrugged his shoulders. "Yeah," he said, more an acknowledgment of the question than a reply to it. "Don't know. Maybe."

CHAPTER 17

Johnny lay in bed, wide awake. He turned on his side, smacked his pillow into a comfortable shape and stared at the clock. Three a.m. Maybe that burger and pie were keeping him up. Or the excitement of what went down at The Hungry One.

After dropping off Billy, he returned to his apartment at one to find Olivia curled up and sleeping on the couch and Shirlee asleep in the bed, the TV on at low volume to CNN. Johnny had shut the TV, stripped down to his boxers and slipped into bed as stealthily as possible. He had fallen asleep quickly, only to open his eyes an hour later.

Nothing external had awakened him. But now nagging thoughts swirled through his head. The 3 a.m. blues. What was Rog's plan? Why did the Death Playas react so violently to Billy rather than laugh it off? How long was Olivia going to be staying here? Were she and Billy breaking up? If they did, how would that affect the band? Could they still work together? Were they ready for the gig at Slim's? Are the new songs he wrote as good as the others? Am I ever going to get out of that job at the bank? The thoughts bounced off each other and repeated themselves until Johnny finally sat up, dangling his feet over the side.

"John," came Shirlee's sleepy voice out of the darkness. "What's the matter? Can't sleep?" She reached a hand from under the blanket and touched his back.

"Yeah. It's nothing. Usual nonsense." He turned to look at her. "Is Livie going back home tomorrow?"

"She said she'll either go back or go to her aunt's place. Decide tomorrow. She's still pretty upset."

"Yeah. Billy said the fight they had was cause he acted like a jerk when Olivia thought she was pregnant."

"Oh shit." Shirlee sat up. "No wonder. She told me that she had been late and thought she was pregnant for a few days, but not about Billy's reaction. Oh, he can sure be an idiot."

"Really," agreed Johnny, thinking of the scene at the biker bar tonight. "He feels terrible about it. I know he misses her."

"Yeah. Hey, did you get into a fight tonight?"

"Not really. A little altercation." He briefly told her what happened earlier. "Why'd you ask?"

"Charles called earlier and was all upset. Said he had a dream where you were surrounded by guys out to get you."

"Huh. Charles is a strange guy."

Yeah, he is." Shirlee curled under the covers, turned over and closed her eyes. "Try to get some sleep, baby."

Johnny laid down and stared at the ceiling, humming the phrase "get some sleep" in his brain like a mantra. He slowly drifted off.

At the same time, Del was standing with Smokey outside of The Hungry One. The gathering place was closed for the night and the neon sign was off. Only a single blue white street light illuminated the parking lot. Standing opposite them in a small triangle formation were three men, dressed in sagging pants and extra large white tee shirts. The guy at the tip of the triangle had long straight brown hair kept in place by a red bandana.

"So what so important you call me out here middle of the night?" the red bandana wearing man said. He was 170, 5' 9', shorter than the bikers, but wiry, with a demeanor that commanded attention and respect. That said "don't fuck with me."

Del told him of the two white guys who came to the club earlier asking about oxy and what had happened. "I figured you'd wanna know, Miguel. And you got pissed the last time I tried to tell you on the phone about…"

"Yeah, yeah," interrupted Miguel. "You did good. You say they recognized your man here from the Whiskey?" Del nodded yes. "Okay then. Don worry bout it. We handle it. For you it's business as usual." He turned and walked to a brown Chevrolet Impala, his two men following behind. They got in and drove off, the darkness quickly swallowing them from sight.

CHAPTER 13

Johnny woke up the next morning to the sounds of dishes clattering and singing coming from the kitchen. With Shirlee still next to him, wrapped up in the blankets, head to toe as if in a cocoon, he knew it must be Olivia. He pulled on the pants and tee shirt he had discarded the night before and walked quietly out of the bedroom, closing the door behind him.

"Coffee?" asked Olivia, raising the half-full coffee pot. She was dressed and ready for the day, white shirt, beige knee length skirt, brown small heeled shoes, eye liner and lipstick applied.

"Sure," replied Johnny, sinking into a chair around the small round kitchen table. A small plate sat on the other side, bread crumbs all that was left of Olivia's breakfast. "You're up early."

"Guess so. Have to get to work. First day at the new job." Olivia took a final sip of coffee and rinsed out the red Abbey Road mug in the sink. She stepped quickly past Johnny at the table to the couch, shaking and folding the blanket. "I'll be out of your hair tonight." She gathered up the clothes she had brought over which were laying on and around the couch- jeans, underwear, sandals, tee shirts—and stuffed them into a backpack. "I think that's it."

"You going back to Billy?" Johnny asked, pleased that he was regaining his place but curious and concerned about his friends.

"I'll call him later," she answered mysteriously, evading the question. Olivia had already made up her mind where she was going from here, at least temporarily, but didn't want to get into it with Johnny right now. Her Aunt Lori always had a bed made and ready for her in her Studio City home and always welcomed Olivia's company. She opened the Uber app on her phone and requested a ride. She looked up at Johnny. "Ten minutes."

"Okay. Remember, we have that gig at Slim's tomorrow night. Seven o'clock set up."

"I got it." She lifted the backpack onto her right shoulder and headed for the apartment door. "Thanks for letting me crash here, Johnny." She gave him a kiss on the cheek. "I'll see you tomorrow. Say bye to Shirlee for me."

"Yeah. Sure." Johnny watched as Olivia went out the door and heard her footsteps echoing down the hallway toward the elevator. Time for me to get ready for work too, he thought. He put his coffee mug on the counter and went into the bedroom to dress.

On the street, Olivia watched as a white Nissan Sentra pulled up to the curb. She leaned into the opened passenger side window. "Oliver?"

"Olivia?" the light brown bearded driver answered.

Olivia opened the backdoor, threw in her backpack and got settled for the drive into Hollywood. She was nervous, first day at the job jitters, but told herself this was a great new opportunity and to make the most of it. She felt cautiously optimistic. After high school, Olivia had attended Valley College, earning her associates degree while working a series of low paying jobs. Sales at Macy's, waitressing at Barone's restaurant, a stint at a dog adoption agency and then manning the front desk at a vet's office in Encino. The pets were cute but after she had to ward off Dr. McConnell's clumsy advances, she realized that she needed a new direction.

It was Shirlee who first made her aware of the paralegal program at UCLA. They had been talking about whether Olivia should sue the vet for sexual harassment when Shirlee mentioned that she should speak to Susan Spadril, a friend of hers who had attended the UCLA program and was now at a major L.A. law firm, Battara and Longflower. Although she decided eventually not to pursue a lawsuit, after the conversation with Spadril Olivia realized that if this woman, who was very pleasant, sweet and helpful but certainly not a world class intellect, could be a paralegal so could she. A year and a half later, Olivia had her paralegal certificate and now had her first job in the field, working in the legal department of the motion pictures group at Paramount Pictures.

She looked at her watch, wondering whether Billy was up yet. I might not get a chance to call him later today at work, she thought, and punched in his number. The phone rang three times and a sleepy voice answered.

"'lo?"

"Billy? You awake? It's Liv."

"Livie?" Billy's voice came to life. "That you, baby?" Excitement crowding out the Jamaican accent.

"Yes, it's me. I know it's early but I wanted to let you know I'm not at Johnny and Shirl's anymore."

"Oh, good. So you'll be home soon then?"

"No. 'member I told you I was starting that new job today."

"Right, yeah. So after work?"

This was the hard part but the real reason she had called now and hadn't put it off until later in the day. "Billy," she said softly. "I'm gonna stay with Aunt Lori for now. Until things get sorted out."

"Sorted out?" said Billy, hurt and anger in his voice. "We can sort it out together. I love you, baby. I told you I'm sorry."

"I know, Billy. But I have to do what's best for me. Give it some time."

"Some time? Man, that's what I've been doing. You oughta come home tonight," he said emphatically.

"No. that's not happening. I'll see you tomorrow night at Slim's."

The phone line went dead as Billy disconnected. He'll get over it, Olivia thought, although she wasn't all that sure.

CHAPTER 13

"Cedars-Sinai Hospital. How may I direct your call?" It had taken Johnny ten minutes to work his way through the automated responses until he was able to get a live person on the phone. It was only another five before his break was over and he'd be back at his station, nodding and smiling at the bank customers.

"Yes. Er, I'd like to speak with one of your patients. Roger Cray." He didn't want to make another trip to the hospital and figured whatever he found out, which wasn't much, he could tell Rog over the phone.

"Cray, hmmm." Johnny could almost see the woman looking over the patient listings as she searched for Rog's extension.

"It was on the fourth floor," he said, trying to be helpful and speed things along.

"Yes sir, I see that he was on the fourth floor. Room 4012. But he's no longer there."

"He's been moved?"

"No. He's left the hospital. Yesterday afternoon."

That took Johnny aback. The nurse had told him that Rog would need to be under doctor's care for at least another few days. He certainly didn't look like he was ready to leave two days earlier.

"He was discharged?" he asked.

"I can't tell you that, sir. Patient confidentiality you understand. Is there anything else I can help you with," the woman said, trying to dismiss him.

Johnny grappled with confusion as he tried to sort out what was happening and what he should do next. He thought of the nurse that had cozied up to Rog. What was her name?

"Torrez," he said, just as the woman was about to disconnect.

"Torrez, sir?"

"Yes, can I speak with Nurse Torrez. She was caring for him."

"I'll connect you with the nurses' station on the fourth floor." A click and a muzak version of "What the World Needs Now is Love, Sweet Love" played on the phone. A minute passed.

"Nurses' station," another woman's voice came on the line.

"Yes," said Johnny, relieved. "Can I speak to Nurse Torrez, please?" Maybe she wouldn't be such a stickler for rules. She had seen him with Rog, he thought, and she was obviously taken with him. Why Johnny didn't know, but, like the saying goes, attraction is a mystery.

"Nurse Torrez is off duty. Would you like to leave a message?"

Damn. "Yeah. This is Johnny Whoop, er Watson, Johnny Watson." He gave her his cell number. "Please ask her to call me. It's about Roger Cray."

"I'll give her the message." The line went dead.

Johnny left the employee break room and went back to his post by the front door, nodding at his supervisor, Teddy, who looked worn down and ancient. Like he had been at his post since California had become a state.

He must be home, Johnny thought. I'll call Shirlee next break, let her know I'll be going into Hollywood when I leave the bank tonight, make sure he's okay.

Four hours later Johnny was driving east on Santa Monica Boulevard, heading toward Hollywood from Beverly Hills. Stopped at a light, a silver Maserati edged up next to his Honda, the driver, neatly trimmed beard, long flowing black hair, chiseled features, might have been in today's Daily Variety. A perfect fit for a car that was ridiculous for driving in Los Angeles' never-ending rush hour. The driver revved the Maserati's engine, raising the decibel to jet plane level. Even with the windows rolled up, Johnny not only heard but felt the vibration. Johnny pressed down on the gas pedal on his car in response, the Honda roaring as loud as its four cylinders allowed and looked over. The driver was laughing and gave Johnny a thumbs up sign.

Past Doheny and into West Hollywood and by The Troubadour nightclub, another music institution, now over fifty years since it opened its doors. Through West Hollywood, the area known as Boys Town, the epicenter of alternative sexual life in greater L.A., and to the major intersection of La Cienega Boulevard, where Johnny turned left and then right onto Fountain Avenue.

Johnny had been to Rog's apartment on Fountain near Wilcox Avenue a few times in the last year, the first being after that great gig when Conflict opened for The Dead Kennedys a little over a year ago. After he and the band had played and everyone stayed and marveled at the power and excitement of the headlining band, the drinks had flowed along with plenty of pot and coke. At two o'clock the club had to close, but Rog invited everyone who was still there over to his place, where the party continued until daylight and breakfast at Canter's Deli on Fairfax.

Johnny pulled into an open parking space in front of the apartment building. On a street formerly filled with one story homes extending from the street back through their narrow lots, many of the houses had been razed and multistory apartment buildings, like this one, had been built among them in the 1990's. The neighborhood was filled with young kids, just getting into Hollywood and looking for that golden ticket, seniors who had lived there since the last golden era of Hollywood and working-class people who could afford the comparably reasonable rent for this area of town, so close to the glitz and glamour only a few blocks away.

Rog's apartment building had a large sign in script letters on the front wall of its four stories, "Fountain Towers." Not quite a tower, Johnny thought. He buzzed the button for Rog's apartment and waited. No response. He buzzed again. Nothing. Not home, I guess, he thought. Strange for someone who had to go everywhere in a wheelchair. Maybe he's staying with a friend.

A red headed girl in her twenties, dressed for a night out in a red cocktail dress, exited the front door of the building. She smiled at Johnny, who, although distracted by the girl for a moment, caught the door before it clicked shut. He rode the elevator to the second floor, exited and walked down the gray carpeted hall, which smelled of spicy food. He knocked on 207. Again no answer.

"Rog?" he called out, directing his voice toward the door. "You in there, man?" He reached down, leaning on the door handle. It turned and Johnny slowly opened the apartment door. "Rog?" He stepped in.

CHAPTER 20

Johnny remembered the now quiet apartment. Two bedrooms, one of which Rog kept as a playroom/office, a kitchen, and a short closeted entryway that led directly into the living room. Not particularly neat, clothes, magazines, CDs were always strewn throughout the place. But not like this.

The cushions on the black leather couch in the center of the living room were on the floor. A glass was overturned, toppled from the marble coffee table, the clear liquid puddling onto the wood floor. Magazines had been swept off the coffee table as well and lay open haphazardly on the floor next to a pair of worn sandals. Two of the three high stools along the bar separating the kitchen from the living room were overturned.

The kitchen drawers were open as were the cupboards, the contents scattered. A couple of coffee cups were shattered on the counter next to the sink. The refrigerator door was ajar, an already opened forty-eight ounce bottle of Coca-Cola on its side, slowly leaking. Other meager items, a few small containers of yogurt, a half loaf of whole wheat bread and a pack of Oscar Meyer salami, were swept to the sides of the shelves.

Johnny hurried around the wall and into the brown

carpeted hallway leading to the bathroom and bedrooms. There were indentations in the carpet, marks of 2 parallel wheels, as in a wheelchair, Johnny thought.

Inside the bedroom, the duvet with a purple madras cover was on the floor, the mattress halfway off the box spring. As in the kitchen, the six drawers in the dresser were open, the shirts, underwear and other items of clothing and keepsakes pushed to the sides or hanging from the edge of the drawers. The sliding door to the closet was open and there was an opening in the middle where the shirts and pants hanging there were pushed to the left and right on the bar. Three pairs of shoes sat on the ground.

In the other bedroom that Rog outfitted as an office, Johnny found the ergonomic chair by the desk on its side, the desk drawers open, paperwork, pens on the floor. The computer that Johnny had seen on the desk was gone, the laptop removed from the setup, cords disconnected. On the wall facing the desk, the books and assorted souvenirs, miniatures of the Eiffel Tower, London Bridge, the Statue of Liberty, were askew in the floor-to-ceiling built-in bookcase. In the center of the bookcase a gap showed and a small steel door was open. Johnny looked inside the safe, finding nothing.

What happened here, thought Johnny. Could Rog have done this? Unlikely since he would have had to stand to create all the chaos, especially in the higher drawers and book shelves. So if not Rog, then who? What were they looking for and did they find it? And where the hell is Rog?

Johnny exited the apartment, his thoughts swirling, making his way toward the stairs at the end of the hall. He and Shirlee had used those stairs that first night here, racing each other out onto the street in the early morning, laughing at the sheer joy of being alive. Plus the high octane weed they had just smoked.

The door to apartment 220 opened and an elderly white man, 5'4", in a flannel bathrobe stepped out, a bag of fragrant garbage in his arms. He passed Johnny without comment. Johnny turned back toward him as the elderly man walked toward the garbage chute at the other end of the hall.

"Sir?" said Johnny. "Excuse me, sir?"

The man stopped and looked over his shoulder at Johnny. "What?" he said in a smoke damaged voice.

"Did you see…"

"Wait a minute," the man said. "This garbage bag is gonna burst." He shuffled down the hall, opened the chute and stuffed the bag in, watching it slide down to the blue bin at the bottom. The chute door clanged shut and the man shuffled back to Johnny. "Now what is it you want?"

"Do you know Roger Cray in 207?"

"The Brit? Yeah, he's been here about two, three years. Why?"

"Have you seen him lately?"

"No. I stay to myself. Don't meddle in other people's affairs, ya know."

"Did you happen to see any people you didn't recognize hanging around this floor, maybe near Mr. Cray's apartment, in the last few days?"

"Hmm, I don't know," he paused. "Come to think of it, there were a couple of scruffy looking characters here yesterday. Didn't know them at all."

"Can you describe them?"

"Scruffy looking," the elderly man repeated. "You know, Mexican."

"Men, women? Young, old?"

"What are you trying to do, be a real cop?" The man eyed his uniform. Johnny had left his hat and gun in the car, but otherwise was dressed for work. "Man, I don't know how old. They all look the same to me. OK? Now you're making me miss the Wheel." He brushed past Johnny, opened his apartment door and closed it behind him.

Johnny went down the stairs and walked to his car. He looked down the street and realized why it had always seemed so familiar to him. It was around the corner from the Hollywood Division of the Los Angeles Police Department. The building where he, Billy, Shirlee and Olivia had been summoned and where they spoke with Detectives Lapidus and Perry last year. Maybe they were there now and could help find Rog.

He walked around the corner and up the wide stone steps of the police precinct. As he reached for the handle of the wood framed glass door, his phone rang. "Hello?" he answered. "Livie. That you?"

"Hi Johnny," came Olivia's voice over the phone. "Shirlee told me you were heading into Hollywood after work. Are you still around?"

"Yeah. About to visit an old friend. What's up?"

"You think you could pick me up at Paramount and drop me in Studio City on your way home?"

Paramount was about a mile from where he stood. "All right. Give me half an hour. Meet me in front of the gates on Melrose."

"Thank, Johnny. Bye."

He put the phone in his pocket and pulled open the door to the station.

CHAPTER 21

Johnny remembered the shoulder high wooden counter ten feet from the entrance and the heavy-set, middle-aged sergeant sitting behind it, looking alert and bored at the same time. "Willis" was the name on the tag pinned over his left breast.

"Hi," said Johnny, putting a smile on his face to convey familiarity and that we're all in this together.

"What can I do for you, son?" said Willis. He gave Johnny and his partial uniform the once over with an amused closed mouth grin.

"I'm looking for Detective Lapidus. Or Detective Perry if she's not here."

"Down the hall, around to the left." Willis dismissed him with a nod of his head.

As Johnny turned down the hall he heard a female voice call out "Johnny. Johnny Watson."

"Detective Connie Lapidus," answered Johnny. He shook her outstretched hand. 5' 4', still about 120 pounds, something looked different about her. "What did you do?"

"The hair," she said, brushing her fingers through the end of her black bob. "A little color, a little cut. A new me." She laughed. "It's been a long time, Junior Detective. What are you doing here?"

"Looking for you. Can we go somewhere to talk? Get a quick coffee?"

"I was heading out, but if you can handle coffee burnt to a crisp, come on back. I have a few minutes."

They walked down the hall into the detectives' area, ten desks only, a few separated by glass partitions and barely enough space between to walk through. At one end was a table with cups, Coffee Mate, packets of sugar and Splenda and a coffee machine, permanently on. The strong, acrid smell wafted up from the coffee pot. Lapidus poured coffee into two paper cups, handed one to Johnny and led him to a desk covered with three neat piles of paperwork of various depths. She sat in the office chair and motioned Johnny to sit in the scuffed chair beside her.

"So tell me what's going on, Johnny."

Johnny told her about the incident at the club and what happened to Rog, visiting him at Cedars, his absence from the hospital today and what he found at Rog's apartment. He hesitated but then told her of his and Billy's visit to the Death Playas and Rog's theory that he had been intentionally injured to open up the drug market at the club. He didn't want to get Rog in trouble with the cops, but if something had happened to him, it was crucial to give Lapidus all the information. Anyway, Rog wasn't dealing now, thought Johnny. So there'd be nothing for Lapidus to charge him with.

"So you just came from there," Lapidus confirmed, adding a note to the yellow pad on which she had been writing. "Was there any evidence of a struggle, any blood?"

"No. No blood. But it's hard to say if there was a struggle. The place looked tossed. Like someone was looking for something." He told her of the open safe.

"Okay. And you say Cray was released from the hospital yesterday?"

"Released or left on his own. They wouldn't tell me which."

Lapidus sighed. "Well," she said. "Cray could have left the hospital, gone through his apartment looking for something and then went to stay with a friend. Does he have family anywhere close by? Or other friends he could be with?"

"No. Not that I know of," said Johnny, disheartened. "You know, I did see wheelchair marks in the carpeting. So he was there after the hospital. What if something bad is going on? Can you check his apartment?"

"Unless there's more evidence of a crime than I have here, I can't." She stood and gathered her purse from the desk. "And the club is out of my jurisdiction. West Hollywood is handled by the county Sheriffs. Listen, if you don't hear from Cray within the next 24 to 48 hours, let me know."

Johnny stood and shook his head in acknowledgment.

"You and the band playing these days?" asked Lapidus as they walked through the hallway toward the station entrance.

He told her of the upcoming show at Slim's. "You remember that place, don't you?"

"Yeah, I do," she said, recalling the incident there. "Take care of yourself, Johnny. And let me know if you don't hear from Cray." She turned and walked to the side of the building toward the police parking lot.

"I will," said Johnny, turning the other way toward Fountain and his parked car. "Say hi to Perry for me," he called out.

Lapidus nodded and disappeared around the corner.

Johnny drove down the street, turned right on Vine, heading south toward Melrose, where he turned east toward downtown. It was 7:30 and traffic moved easily now that the main thrust of the rush hour had passed. The soundstages of Paramount Pictures were quickly visible and Johnny made a left into the gated entrance to the studio, swinging a U-turn in the driveway. A uniformed guard opened the door to the security post and began to approach the Honda when Olivia, who had been standing on the sidewalk looking at her phone, opened the passenger door. The guard retreated, waving toward Johnny and they pulled back into the flow of traffic, heading west.

"Thanks for picking me up, Johnny," said Olivia. "Saved me from having to pay for another Uber ride."

"Yeah, that's okay. But you're gonna have to figure out something now that you're working here. You can't be bumming rides and Ubering all the time." He turned right onto Gower, heading north, the Hollywood hills ahead of them.

"I know. I'll get a car. Maybe I'll move down here. There are decent places near here and I could walk to work."

"Yeah, you could. Shirlee told me you and Billy had a fight about that." Olivia nodded. "But Billy told me a different story." He hesitated, before deciding to convey what Billy had said. "That you told him you were pregnant and he freaked out, only to find out later that you weren't."

"He told you that?"

"Yeah. Why'd you make up a story for Shirlee? I thought she was your best friend."

She is," insisted Olivia. "I just didn't want her getting in the middle of it. Especially with you and Billy being so tight."

"It's understandable for you to be pissed at him for going nuts when he thought you were pregnant. More than fighting over moving to Hollywood," said Johnny. He turned left on Franklin and accelerated up the ramp at Argyle onto the Hollywood Freeway.

"There was no reason for him to act like that," she said indignantly. "We've been together all these years. What did he think would eventually happen?"

"But it didn't happen," corrected Johnny.

"Well, it could've. At anytime." She went silent, purposely avoiding Johnny's sideways glances, staring out the window. Johnny turned on the radio, "Lonely Boy" by the Black Keys contrasting and illuminating the mood in the car.

Johnny drove over the hills out of Hollywood and down into the San Fernando Valley. He exited at Laurel Canyon Boulevard, made a series of turns and stopped in front of Olivia's aunt's home.

Olivia opened the passenger door and stepped out, her backpack over her left shoulder.

"Thanks again for the ride," she said, closing the car door.

"Sure. Don't forget about the gig tomorrow."

"Yeah." She turned and walked up the path to the house.

Johnny watched her Aunt Lori open the door, hug her and let Olivia in. Johnny waved at Lori, who waved back and closed the door to the house. Johnny drove off.

CHAPTER 22

Olivia drove herself to Slim's the next night, choosing not to pile into the SUV with Johnny, Billy and Frank. Although the SUV was technically hers, Billy was in possession of it and she didn't want to get into a fight about that too.

Her Aunt Lori let her borrow her car, a black 2016 Kia Forte. Small but functional, it was fine for Olivia's purposes, hauling her and her cymbal bag and kit bag, full of drum sticks, bass pedal, bandages, tape, drum keys and assorted pads and accessories, to the gig. Fortunately Slim's had a decent back line, including amps for the guitars and bass and an old, rickety Pearl drum set. Hundreds, maybe thousands of drummers had pounded away at that thing, but it was still standing.

Lankershim Boulevard wasn't far from Lori's house, just a few overly familiar miles. Olivia's mind wandered as she drove, not concentrating on the traffic or the route. She knew that Billy would probably ask her to come back to his apartment after the gig. She did have her clothes and belongings there. But going back tonight would mean more to Billy than simply spending the night. It would mean they were together again and everything was fine. And it wasn't as far as she was concerned.

They had been together, on and off, for so long, it had become hard for either one of them to think of themselves as separate, independent of each other. For almost ten years now, it had been Billy and Olivia, Livie and Billy. Except for those times when she had walked out before. Like when he decided after high school that the way to stardom was to busk on the streets of London, a latter day Paul Simon, only to come back a month later, broke, hungry and begging her to let him in and take him back. Or when he thought he could make out with that traitor bitch Giselle without any thought of the consequences.

I wasn't always so dependent on him, she thought, equating him with me, him and me as us. That's not how my parents raised me, to be filled with anxiety if things weren't going right with a boy.

Her mother, Vanessa Sanders Felton, was originally from Boston and had been a photojournalist with an active career, contributing photos to Life Magazine, National Geographic and other magazines and newspapers. Before she married, she accepted assignments overseas, shooting the fall of the Berlin wall and the dissolution of the Soviet Union. In Los Angeles to cover the aftermath of the 1994 Northridge earthquake, she met Steven Felton, an orthopedic surgeon from Los Angeles who was working in a hospital in Tarzana where quake casualties were brought. After instant attraction and a feverish courtship, accelerated no doubt by the drama and excitement they were experiencing in Los Angeles in those trying times, they married. Oliva was born soon after. Not wanting to miss out on her baby daughter's formative years, Vanessa decided to work out of Los Angeles and raise her beautiful little star.

And in every way, Olivia was that, Vanessa and Steven's little star. Smart, beautiful from infancy, and filled with confidence either inborn or bred from having two parents telling her how special she was from a young age, Oliva was a force to be reckoned with. Olivia was a straight "A" student throughout school, studied classical piano for five years beginning when she was six and had a burgeoning modeling career as a young teenager. Her mother had begun taking photos of her when only a baby and had shown some of Olivia at 12 to a friend at an ad agency. Photo shoots for face cream, shampoo and designer clothing followed, which segued to commercials.

But all that stopped when she met Billy Bates in her junior year in high school. After that it was all about hanging out with the quirky, charismatic musician. He introduced her to rock, rap, reggae and blues music, giving her an education in styles of music that had been missing from the home she grew up in. He also introduced her to drugs, a little pot at first and then experimentation with other mind-altering substances. Her interest in school declined. Her grades suffered and Vanessa and Steven's dreams of an Ivy League college education for their daughter disappeared. It led to some major battles on the home front for Olivia, her parents not understanding what she saw in the blond haired musician with the bogus Jamaican accent. But Olivia didn't care at the time. Love would conquer all.

Until it didn't, she thought, turning down the alley way and parking in the small lot behind the club. Those thoughts swirled around her head, distracting her and causing her to feel uneasy about seeing Billy and the rest of the band as she stepped out of the Kia. Johnny was reaching inside the Subaru SUV, parked two spots over, and pulled out his guitar case and pedal board. Frank was entering the back door of the club as Billy came around the vehicle from the driver's side.

"Hey, dahlin'," he said, coming toward her. Billy dropped his guitar case on the asphalt surface of the parking lot and moved in to kiss her on the lips. She shifted her head and his lips brushed her cheek.

"Hi Billy," Olivia said, forcing a tight lipped smile. "What time do we go on, Johnny?"

"Oh, you know. Around 8:30 but whenever we're ready to roll," said Johnny, swinging the door open, placing his foot to stop it and stepping inside, his arms full. Olivia hurriedly followed him in, Billy trailing behind.

CHAPTER 23

The club was dark and intimate. The back door led onto a small dance area, linoleum floor, bright yellow, red and blue lights above, in front of an even smaller raised wooden stage, a single foot off the ground. Frank was on stage in the corner, plugging in his bass and adjusting the sound. Billy, Johnny and Olivia joined him, Johnny unpacking and setting up his pedal board, a sequenced added sound system to give his guitar any number of sonic effects. Billy plugged into a Marshall amp, a single wah wah pedal at his feet. Olivia took the cymbals out of the leather case she carried them in and placed them on the three cymbal stands surrounding the house drums.

"Hey guys. And girl," said a middle-aged dark haired guy, coming up to the stage, rubbing his hands. "Ready for a good show tonight?"

"Yeah, Eddie," replied Billy. "You know we be good." He turned away from him, concentrating on tuning his guitar.

"What's his noise?" Eddie asked Johnny, who shrugged.

"Personal problems," said Johnny, unplugging and replugging a cord into one of the small rectangular boxes at his feet.

"Hey, no personal problems here, okay?" said Eddie. "Just give me a good show. All right?"

"Sure, Eddie," said Johnny. "We won't let ya down."

"Okay," said Eddie. "Ya got half an hour. One drink a piece." He handed Johnny four tickets, redeemable at the bar.

Eddie had opened the club five years ago after working as a bartender at bars and clubs throughout Los Angeles, New York and London. Impressed by the dynamic scene at CBGBs in New York he had tried to foster an open atmosphere for young musicians and other artists, opening his door not only to bands of all styles of music, but other performers, including poets, spoken word artists, dancers, performance artists, actors reciting scenes, just about anyone who wanted a stage. Of course, if they brought a bunch of friends with them, drinking friends especially, well, then you might get a return invitation and become one of Eddie's favorites.

Conflict had been elevated to that lofty perch a couple of years ago. The band had always brought at least a small crowd right from the first time they played. Shirlee and Olivia, who wasn't in the band at that time, did the work to get friends to check out Johnny and Billy's musical project. And though the group had transferred most of their gigs to the Whiskey in the last year, Slim's was their home away from home, making it an easy choice for introducing new material or just jamming for an hour in front of mostly friends.

Olivia finished setting up, jumped off the stage and threaded her way past the early arriving crowd to the bar. She had on her favorite outfit, red skirt that flared out when she moved, a white Runaways tee shirt featuring a picture of the members of that 1970s all-female Los Angeles band, and red platform shoes. The bartender noticed her approach before she sat down on one of the stools lining the bar.

"Livia, darlin, ya lookin good," said Serge, in his Eastern European accent, making a show of wiping the bar in front of her. "Drink?"

"Vodka and cranberry," she said, handing Serge her one free drink coupon.

"One for me too," said a female voice behind her. Olivia turned to see Shirlee smiling at her. She was still dressed in her Norm's waitressing uniform, although it did not seem out of place. "How are you, Livie? Getting fortified?"

"Oh, she's gonna need more than that," said a tenor voice to Olivia's right. Charles was dressed in purple pants, a ruffled white shirt and a purple beret. "You were in my dreams last night and fireworks were going off all around you."

"Well, in that case," said Olivia, raising her glass and clinking with Shirlee. "Here's to fortification." She took a sizable swallow, draining half the liquid in the highball glass.

"Hey, Livie," said Shirlee, moving in close so that Charles on the other side of Olivia couldn't hear. "Johnny told me what really sparked your fight with Billy. Why didn't you tell me instead of that story about moving to Hollywood?"

"That story was true," stated Olivia, annoyance in her voice. "We did argue about moving into Hollywood. And I felt stupid about the false pregnancy. The whole damn argument wouldn't have happened if I hadn't said anything until I knew for sure."

"Yeah," said Shirlee, rubbing her finger on the rim of the glass. "But he still shouldn't have reacted that way."

"Right? He was a real asshole."

"Who?" asked Charles, having heard Olivia's raised voice. "Who's an asshole?"

"You, dreamboy," said Shirlee, pushing him playfully in the arm.

"Olivia!" came Billy's voice over the public address system from the stage. "Let's play."

She finished the last of her drink. "Duty calls." She stood, glanced at the stage where Billy was searching the crowd for her, sighed and, head down, walked back through the audience, which had now packed the small venue.

"Woo, woo!" Catcalls greeted her as she jumped on the stage. She winked and wiggled her fingers at the crowd, positioning herself behind the drums. She scooped up a pair of sticks from the floor and looked to Johnny who was facing the band, his back to the crowd.

"Ready?" he asked. Nods all around. "Okay. 'School of Dreams.'" He turned to the audience. "This one's for a friend of ours." He signaled Olivia with a shake of his head.

"…2, 3, 4."

Billy played a hesitating, rhythmic lead guitar line and the rest of the group played the same notes with him, creating a powerful opening phrase that grabbed the audience's attention right away. They repeated it twice and let the last note hang in the air. Johnny sang.

"There's nothing to know, nothing to teach." Billy repeated the last four notes sung on guitar.

"Nowhere to search, nobody to reach.

"Everyone looks for that special thing.

"I look for you in my dreams."

Billy repeated the opening line, this time with the band playing a languid but surging rhythm, like the tide coming in on a cloudy day.

"I look for you in my dreams.

"Secrets are kept, life in-between.

"The vision is red, life is a scheme.

"I look for you in my dreams."

Billy repeated the last four notes again and launched into a solo. The band pulsed behind him, provided a wall of sound, supporting Billy's playing, Frank playing those four notes over and over again on bass, Johnny thrashing power chords, Olivier pounding straight quarter notes.

Billy continued, the solo extending. Johnny looked at him, but Billy was in the zone, mesmerized by his own playing and the sound surrounding him. Sweat erupted onto his forehead and dripped onto the stage. He wailed, a piercing solo, his fingers running all the way up the neck of his guitar. The entire audience was fixed on him as was the band, watching him for a cue, for a return to the last verse of the song. Billy turned in his reverie and looked at Olivia, catching her eye. He winked at her and licked his lips suggestively.

Olivia mouthed the words "Fuck you." It was unmistakable.

In one quick movement, Billy detached his guitar strap and swung his guitar, smashing it into one of the cymbal stands, the cymbal crashing into the drum set, narrowly missing Olivia. She fell backwards off the drum stool, against the wall inches behind her. From the floor of the stage, Olivia yelled "Asshole!" and flung the drum sticks at Billy, hitting him in the face.

Johnny and Frank stopped playing, too stunned to continue. The show must go on, but there was a different show going on now. The crowd watched in silence, like gawkers at the site of a car crash. Olivia stood, shoved Billy off the stage as she strode past and exited the side door, slamming the door behind her. Billy began to run after her but stopped when he felt a hand on his arm.

"Leave her be, Billy" said Shirlee. "Leave her alone."

CHAPTER 24

"That asshole," yelled Olivia, tears running down her cheeks, fury in her eyes. Shirlee stood next to the Kia in Slim's parking lot, not saying anything, letting Olivia vent her emotions from the driver's seat. "What the fuck was he thinking? Acting like that to me now? Did he think that was gonna make me want him again? The hot shot guitarist? What am I, some groupie in front of the stage at a fuckin Kiss show, salivating over Gene Simmons? Is he 25 or 15? What a jerkoff!"

"You know he wasn't thinking," said Shirlee, barely suppressing a smile at the description. "When either of those guys get into it like that, the id takes over. That guitar becomes an extension of their dicks."

Olivia burst out laughing. "Oh my god," she exclaimed. "How pathetic." She looked in her rearview mirror at her reflection. "What a mess. Jesus. I'm sorry, Shirl. I've gotta go." She started the car's engine.

"Call me tomorrow," said Shirlee as Olivia backed the Kia out of the parking spot. "Or anytime." Olivia straightened the car and drove down the alley toward the street.

"Where's she going?" asked Johnny, who had come out of the club to check on the girls. "Eddie wants us to finish at least one set."

"Eddie will have to do it himself," Shirlee said. "Or you can play without a drummer."

"I think we're done for the night then," said Johnny. "Billy's a wreck. I'll let Eddie know we're packin it in for the night."

Inside the crowd had dissipated and dissolved, only a few stragglers, Eddie and Serge remaining. Billy sat with Frank in a booth, quietly talking and nursing drinks. Shirlee and Johnny shoved in next to them. Serge opened two PBRs and Eddie walked them to the booth, handing the beers to Johnny and Shirlee.

"That's it for the night, Eddie," said Johnny. "Livie's gone."

"Yeah, that's okay," said Eddie. "Some nights are like that." He retreated to the bar and drained a shot glass of brown liquid.

CHAPTER 25

Tim stepped aside as Miguel and his dos hermanos walked into the club. Miguel had never been inside the Whiskey before, hardly ever ventured this far west unless business demanded it. But he remembered hearing stories from his Uncle Rico about seeing Los Lobos here in the 1980's, about the diverse scene as punks and hipsters from all across Los Angeles congregated to hear one of the top musical acts of the day.

It was obvious the act on stage was no Los Lobos. The crowd was slight, only about a dozen people milling about, half sipping drinks and yelling into each other's ears, half staring bored at the two young white boys sending up waves of sonic distortion, electronic bashing and a few seemingly random musical notes from the twin computers in front of them. The boys' heads bounced as they rode the wave. Unfortunately no one else bounced along.

"Come on," said Miguel, walking up the stairs to the balcony and the second floor offices. "Let's find Les." They went down the hall, Miguel knocked once on the closed office door and stepped inside. Smokey was on the other side of the door, ready to repel boarders, to stop whoever had the nerve to walk into the office without his okay, only to back off when he saw who it was.

"Miguel," Smokey greeted him as the three men walked in. "Les, this here is Miguel."

"Hey," said Les, vaulting out of his seat behind his desk, wiping some loose white powder from his nose. "Miguel, glad to meet you finally." He offered his hand. Miguel looked at it as if it was a poisonous snake.

"Yeah," said Miguel. "You Les, no? I need to know about the two Anglos from last week, the ones who got into a beef in the alleyway with my nephew."

"Oh yeah," began Les. "Those…"

"That was your nephew?" interrupted Smokey. "I thought it was just some little rip off chooch."

One of Miguel's men turned suddenly and put a hand to Smokey's throat. He squeezed, cutting off Smokey's air.

"Don be sayin nasty things about mi familia," threatened Miguel. He nodded at his man, who released his grip, sending Smokey to the floor, gasping.

"Take it easy, brother," said Les, his hands outstretched, trying to calm things down.

"I ain't your brother," said Miguel. "Now who were those gringos?"

"Two musicians," said Les. "In a band called Conflict. They came in here looking for a gig."

"Del said they were asking him for a gig also," said Smokey, recovered but standing more than an arms-length apart from the three Latinos. "Before they asked about drugs."

"Okay," said Miguel. He turned and exited the office, the two men with him following. "Let's find these pendejos," he said to his men as they walked out into the night on Sunset Boulevard.

CHAPTER 26

It had been a long night for everyone, except for Frank who had left soon after the explosion on stage, naturally with his arm around the waist of a young girl he picked out from the crowd. Johnny and Shirlee left Slim's after 1 a.m, having downed several beers and listening at length to Billy alternately bemoaning about how much of an idiot he was and berating Olivia for being unreasonable.

"Unreasonable?" Shirlee had said. "Was swinging your axe at Livie a reasonable thing to do?"

"Yeah, Billy," Johnny had jumped in. "You're not hitting on all cylinders lately. First the incident at that bar the other night and now this? What's with you?"

"I don't know," Billy had replied. "She got me all twisted up." He wiped his reddened eyes with his forearm. "Oh man. What am I gonna do?"

No one had a solution for Billy's situation, no remedies to repair the damage done to Billy's and Olivia's relationship. The best Johnny could offer were platitudes that they had been through tough times before and gotten through it and would again. And Shirlee had offered their couch rather than have Billy go home to a lonely, empty apartment.

Johnny woke the next morning, fixed a cup of coffee and realized it had been a couple of days since he had spoken to Detective Lapidus about Rog. He called Rog's landline number on the chance that he had returned to the apartment. The phone rang with no answer and no voice mail connection. Johnny hung up.

"Who ya callin?" asked Billy, walking into the kitchen from the living room, bare chested in his black Calvin Klein underwear.

"Put some clothes on, man. Shirlee'll be up in a minute."

"Okay, all right." Billy retreated to the couch and slipped on the jeans and black tee shirt from last night. "But who ya callin?" he called from the living room.

"Tryin to get ahold of Rog. He was so eager to find out who was taking over his business and now he's nowhere to be found."

"Plus he owes us some money, right?"

"Who owes you money?" asked Shirlee, stepping through the bedroom door, tucked inside a terry cloth white bathrobe.

"Rog," answered Johnny again. He had told Shirlee about Rog's disappearance and visit to the Hollywood LAPD station after returning home two nights ago.

"If he's still missing, maybe it's time to call your detective friend," said Shirlee. Lapidus and her partner Perry had been instrumental in resolving the mystery of Harry's death and the crucial moments and events leading to the arrest of Mr. Big. Along the way, Johnny, the security guard/musician and Lapidus, the LAPD detective second grade, had formed a bond. Lapidus and Perry had even seen the band play a few times, to Johnny the greatest compliment someone could pay him.

Johnny dialed Lapidus' cell phone number.

"Lapidus," she answered after one ring. "What's up, Watson? Ever hear from your buddy?

"No, Detective. What do you think I should do?"

"Well, since you had said his apartment door was left open, Perry and I paid an unofficial visit the other night. Do you know if he had a girlfriend? Someone named Sylvia Lopez?"

"No. It wouldn't surprise me though. He seems to like Latinas." Johnny thought of Rog with Nurse Torrez. "Why do you ask?"

"Perry found her name and address in Cray's bedside drawer. We looked up her number and left a message but haven't heard back. Not surprising really. Not too many people voluntarily call the cops back when we make a blind call."

"Can you give me that address and phone number? Maybe she'll speak to me." Lapidus relayed the information and Johnny wrote it on a pad on the kitchen counter. "Thanks, Detective. I'll let you know if I find out anything."

"Okay, Watson. Watch yourself." Lapidus disconnected.

Johnny drained the last of the cold coffee, grimaced at the taste and walked into the bedroom to dress for work. As he put on his uniform, he called out.

"You going to work, Billy?"

"Later. Store don open til 'leven. I'll head home first, shower and change. Don't wan da public be offended from da foul smellin tee shirt salesman."

Ten minutes later, Billy and Johnny were both heading out the door, Johnny into Beverly Hill, Billy to his apartment in Reseda. Johnny hugged Shirlee on the way out.

"I might be late again," he said to her. "Can you call Olivia, see how she's doing? I don't know if we have a band at the moment."

"I will," said Shirlee, kissing him on the lips. "Don't worry. And be careful, Mr. Security Guard."

Shirlee went back to the kitchen, toasted a slice of bread and drizzled a healthy portion of honey on the toast. Her schedule at work was erratic, changing week to week. This week she had today free and she relaxed, switching the TV on. Al Roker was announcing today's elderly birthdays. Her cell phone rang.

"Hey Livie," she answered. "Just thinkin of calling you. On the way to work?"

"Hi Shirl. Yeah. Ya know, first week on the job. Wanna be there early if I can."

"Right. How are you feeling? You were pretty upset last night."

"I know. I was. Sorry. Didn't mean to lose it like that. My god, that boy can make me see red." Olivia paused and Shirlee heard her exhaling. "Listen. Tell Johnny I'm sorry, okay?"

"Yeah, of course. You're sticking with the band, right?"

"Right now, I'm not sure of anything. I'm surprised Billy hasn't reached out."

"Do you want him to? We told him to leave you be."

"Oh. Yeah. I guess that's best. I gotta go. Thanks, Shirl."

"Okay, Livie. Later." The line went dead. Shirlee changed channels.

CHAPTER 27

It was early evening and the sun was setting by the time Johnny was able to leave work, throw his badge, cap and gun in the trunk of the Honda and make his way east, down La Cienega Boulevard and onto the 10 Freeway heading toward downtown. He had earlier tried the phone number for Sylvia Lopez with the same result as Lapidus had gotten. No answer, only a female voice saying, "Hola, leave a message." Johnny had done so, reciting his phone number and that he was a friend of Rog's. Now he was heading to Lopez' address on La Verne Avenue in East Los Angeles, an area populated mostly by Hispanics and not yet subject to the rapid gentrification that was spreading across the city.

Keeping his eye on traffic as he navigated through the still thick line of cars on the five lane freeway, he tried Rog's home phone number again, pressing the numbers with one hand, one hand on the wheel. He tucked the ringing phone between his shoulder and ear and listened to the ringing. No answer. Johnny dropped his right shoulder, the phone fell onto his lap and he disconnected. Hopefully Lopez will be at this address and she'll have some answers, thought Johnny.

He tuned the radio to KCRW, the National Public Radio station for Santa Monica, and listened to the nightly news report while he worked his way east. After forty-five minutes he was finally past downtown, into Boyle Heights and transitioning onto the intersecting 5 Freeway. Ten minutes later he was exiting onto East Olympic Boulevard, a mostly industrial section of one of the longest streets in the greater Los Angeles area, stretching from the ocean east to the town of Montebello. Johnny made two Waze-mandated turns and was driving on La Verne Avenue. Small, mostly well-tended houses lined the street, a few outliers with cars on the lawns breaking up the symmetry of green grass leading to small exterior porches.

Johnny pulled in front of number 1412. The house was painted white, the porch, enclosed by screens, was lime green. He exited the car. The street was quiet except for a few passing cars. The sun had set and lights inside houses showed people watching TV, cooking or eating dinner. A heavy-set man was seated in a rocking chair across the street, moving back and forth, drinking a can of beer.

Johnny walked up the asphalt driveway to a connecting paved path, which led to the two steps up to the front door on the porch. He knocked, an assertive three times, and waited. Nobody came to the door of the house, which Johnny could see three feet inside the porch. He found a doorbell on the wooden frame, pressed it and heard it ring inside. Still nothing.

He walked down the steps and to the left side of the house. A five foot high wooden gate, its white paint chipped, divided and blocked the driveway. Johnny peered over and saw a closed garage and another gate to the right, leading to the back of the house.

"Hello?" he called. "Anyone here?"

"Who you looking for?" he heard from a voice behind him. Johnny turned and saw the man from the house across the street standing at the top of the driveway, beer can still in his hand.

"Oh, hi," Johnny said, walking toward the man. He stood about 5' 8 and was wearing loose fitting black sweatpants and a muscle tee-shirt. In his mid-40's he had a thick black mustache, a shaved head and even from this distance, Johnny could see tattoos covered his large forearms. "Does Sylvia Lopez live here?"

"Who's asking?" the man asked, his face a mask void of expression. He drained the last of the beer, crushed the can, turned and tossed it underhand back onto his lawn. It bounced once and landed on his porch.

"I'm Johnny Watson. I'm looking for a friend of mine. And the name Sylvia Lopez and this address was on a piece of paper in his apartment." Now that they stood within a few feet of each other, Johnny saw one of the tattoos on the man's forearms was the word "SUR."

"She's not here," the man said. "Who's your friend?" He squinted his eyes, examining Johnny and waiting for an answer.

"Rog, uh Roger Cray. Maybe you've seen him here? Middle-aged, chunky built, blond hair, English accent."

"No. Don know him."

"Okay," said Johnny. "Thanks." He walked past the man, toward his car.

"Hey, Mr. Johnny. You a cop? Looks like you wearin some kinda uniform," the man said, motioning up and down Johnny's body with his index finger.

Johnny stopped and turned. "No, not a cop. I work private security. They make us wear a uniform."

"Ah," said the man. "Comfort to the customers, scare the bad guys, right?"

Johnny shrugged his shoulders. "Maybe."

"Listen, where can I reach you? I tell Sylvia to call you when she get home."

Johnny thought about it. He finally said, "That's okay. I left a message on her voice mail. Thanks anyway." He turned and walked back to his car, opening the door and sliding in.

The man watched him drive off, down La Verne toward Olympic. He pulled a cell phone out of his pants pocket and pressed a number.

"Miguel? Hey, it's Chuy. Yeah. You were right. I think I found one of your gringos."

CHAPTER 23

"Detective Lapidus, please," Johnny said into his phone as soon as he made the turn onto the freeway on ramp. He merged into traffic heading west, looking for the 5 intersection going north and into the valley.

"This is Lapidus," came the voice over the phone.

"Hi Detective," said Johnny. "It's Watson. I went by that address for Sylvia Lopez. Nobody home, but a very imposing guy from across the street was really interested in what I was doing there. Had major tats with 'S-U-R' in bold on his arm."

"S-U-R? You sure?" asked Lapidus.

"Definitely. What's it mean?"

"It means you've stepped into a landmine, Watson. That's a tattoo for the Sureños 13 gang or SUR 13. Affiliated with the Mexican Mafia. Major trouble."

"Drug dealers?" Johnny knew the answer immediately upon asking the question.

"And then some. Major players," answered Lapidus. "You better steer clear of them. I don't know what your friend Rog has been up to, but it's not good. We'll file a missing person on Cray, but you should stay away, let us handle it."

"OK, Detective. Will you let me know if anything turns up?"

"Sure, Johnny. I'll be in touch." Lapidus disconnected and Johnny tossed his phone onto the passenger seat.

Johnny drove up the 5, connected with the Ventura Freeway going west, eager to get home after a long day. Where could Rog be? he asked himself, but anywhere was the only answer he could muster. Did that gang grab him? Because of drug sales at the club? But Rog isn't even there anymore. Les and his bikers have taken over. Maybe Rog just took off, wanting to get away. Maybe wanting to get out of the line of fire. Johnny couldn't come up with a satisfactory answer. I guess I'm not that great of a detective after all, he thought.

His cell phone rang. It was Shirlee's number.

"Hey baby," he said, answering. "What's up?"

"Are you gonna be home soon?" Shirlee asked. Johnny could hear the worry in her voice.

"Yeah. On my way. Passing Forest Lawn now."

"Forest Lawn? Were you in Glendale?"

"I'll tell you later. What's the matter?"

"It's Billy. Olivia was visiting and he came by to see you. Now both of them are here and it's not going so well. Can you hurry?"

"Be there in 10 minutes."

He transitioned onto the 405 heading north five minutes later, exited at Roscoe and pulled in front of the apartment house in Panorama City. He jumped out, entered the apartment building and went up to his place, anxiously opening the door. He stepped into a storm.

"But I didn't mean anything by it, I swear." Billy was protesting, pleading his case to Olivia. "It was the heat of the moment."

"Don't tell me that," said Olivia emphatically. "You know

how upset I was with you. You couldn't just cool it for once, Mr. Chill Rasta Man?"

"You know there's nothing chill about my feelings for you, Livie," Billy answered, trailing her around the small living room as she furiously paced.

"You shoulda thought of that before you sent that cymbal crashing within an inch of my face!" shouted Olivia, turning on Billy. "Just leave me alone!" She began to cry and Shirlee rushed to her side, holding and comforting her.

"Livie…" Billy began, but Johnny stepped between him and Olivia.

"Come on, man," Johnny said. "Let's take a walk." He guided Billy out the apartment door and into the night. It was cool for L.A., in the 50s and the sky was clear. They walked down the street toward the Plant, a major retail outlet on north Van Nuys Boulevard and the former site of a General Motors assembly plant. Billy took a joint out of his inside jacket pocket and lit it with a purple disposable lighter. He took a hit and offered it to Johnny, who took a drag and returned it.

"I told you to leave her be, man," said Johnny.

"I know," said Billy, taking another hit. In a strangled voice he said, "I didn't mean to. But what was I supposed to do? I came by to talk to you and wham. There she was. I couldn't help myself. Aw shit." He exhaled a thick plume of smoke. "I'm so fucked."

"Take it easy, man. Don't go all drama queen on me now." Johnny opened his eyes as wide as he could, giving Billy a melodramatic look that caused Billy to burst out laughing. "Yeah. Now that's more like the white rasta I know."

Upstairs, Shirlee had opened a bottle of Chardonnay from Costco and she poured them each a second glassful.

"You're a life saver, Shirl," said Olivia, taking a sip. "Man, he is so intense."

"Yeah, the inner tormented Valley boy comes out, right?"

"You know he still goes every week to see his Mom at the retirement home, no matter what."

"How is Mary?" asked Shirlee. She had heard stories from Billy and Johnny about Billy's mother and knew she had Alzheimer's disease.

"She's in but mostly she's out. But Billy's always there. Every week."

"And usually with you," said Shirlee. "You do really care for him." Thinking of Billy's mother made Shirlee think of her own mother. She hadn't spoken and been in contact with her for years now. Blame that letch of a stepfather for that.

A deep sigh from Olivia brought Shirlee out of her reverie. "I do. But he's so infuriating. I just have to take time away from him for now. Stay at Aunt Lori's place, save some money from the job."

"How's that goin?" Shirlee took another drink.

"It's great. Imagine me working at a motion picture studio?" Olivia chuckled in wonder.

"See any stars yet?" asked Shirlee, draining her glass and considering and dismissing another for the moment.

"No," said Olivia. "Unless you count Forrest Gump's bench."

"I'd like to see that," said Johnny, entering the apartment and shutting the door behind him. "You okay, Livie?"

"She's fine," Shirlee answered for her. "Where's Billy?"

"Headed home," Johnny said. "He'll be okay."

"I better get going too," said Olivia, placing her glass on the coffee table and standing. "Sorry about the histrionics earlier, guys." She bent and kissed Shirlee on the cheek.

"Forget it," said Johnny, opening the door for her. She hugged Johnny, turned and left the apartment.

They watched her exit the building from the window. Oliva opened the door to the Kia, started the engine and pulled away.

"You think she'll stay with the band?" Johnny asked Shirlee.

"I don't know, baby. We'll find out soon."

CHAPTER 29

"So he's a cop?" asked one of Miguel's men, wiping green salsa from his mouth.

"Not a cop, Memo," said Chuy. "A security guard." They sat at an outside table under a green umbrella blocking the sun at a local taco place in Whittier called Chema's, a favorite of Miguel's.

"Weren't you listening?" Miguel reprimanded Memo. "Or you too busy stuffing your face?"

"Lo siento, Patrón," said Memo, putting down the king sized chile verde burrito in his hands and giving a sideways glance to the other of Miguel's men. Kique stopped just as he was about to take another bite of a taco and looked furtively at Memo, raising his hand to indicate "what?"

"What did this security guard look like?" asked Miguel, sipping on a straw.

"You know," said Chuy. "Anglo kid, six feet, one seventy, black hair a little long."

"What about the uniform?" asked Miguel. "Any name?"

"No, no name," answered Chuy. "But it had a patch. A plane, a train and a truck in a triangle."

"Okay," said Miguel. "That's good. Should be easy to figure out who he works for. Don need any kid poking round in our business." He finished his horchata and tossed the cup into the nearby trash can. He stood and the other three men all stood as well. "Kique, call Sylvia. Make sure things are quiet."

"Si, Patrón" responded Kike. He stepped away from the table and punched in a number on his phone. It rang twice and a woman's voice answered.

"Yes?"

"It's Kique. Is everything under control there?"

"Oh, sí Mama," said Sylvia. "So nice of you to call. Everything is fine. And how is mija doing?"

"Bueno. Stay there til we tell you to come home." Kique disconnected. "Everything's quiet," he said to Miguel, who acknowledged the information with a shake of his head.

The four men slid into the brown Chevy parked in front of the stand and drove down Whittier Boulevard.

"Was that your mom, Sylvia?" asked Rog, stretched out on a worn brown cloth-covered couch, the cast running down his leg extending to the opposite end, his foot on the arm rest. The room was rustic, wood paneled, stone fireplace. The kitchen and dining room, consisting of a gas oven with four burners and a small table with four wooden, slightly splintering chairs, were alongside the living area without a wall separating the rooms. A twenty-inch TV was on in front of the couch, broadcasting a daytime baseball game.

"Si, amor," replied Sylvia Lopez, formerly known as Nurse Torrez to Rog. It had been easy to convince him that Torrez was her married name from her long-divorced husband and Lopez was her maiden name which she used everywhere except work. The possibility that it was all fake never occurred to el hombre britanico. She wore a pair of tight-fitting jeans and a white blouse that did little to hide her full breasts. "Just making sure everything was ok."

"No problems with your little tike?"

"No, no, mija is fine. She loves her abuela. Do you need a blanket? It can get cold up here." She moved toward the couch, carrying a bright red patterned Indian blanket from the closet, which she shook out. The blanket settled onto Rog. He reached up to her and pulled her onto the couch, nuzzling her breasts.

"Oh, you must be feeling better," she said, laughing and cupping his face with her hands. "I thought you were watching the Dodgers."

"I could never really enjoy this American game. Especially when there are other fun things to do."

A half hour later, Rog was asleep and Sylvia was on the porch of the small cabin, smoking a cigarette and staring off toward the woods. Only a two-hour drive from Los Angeles, Lake Arrowhead was a world apart. A mountain retreat in the San Bernadino National Forest, the town itself was small and quiet. Big Bear, an hour further up the mountain, attracted the winter skiers and the summer party people. Lake Arrowhead was for families with second homes, vacationers, ice skaters with its well-known training facility and people just looking to get away from the intensity of city living. Or, like Sylvia and Rog, looking to just get lost. Hidden throughout the thick woods were A-frames, large and small, as well as basic wooden cabins similar to the one Sylvia looked out from. Adjacent to the town was the lake itself, a recreational area for fishing and small motorboats.

Sylvia didn't have a view of the lake from the porch. Only the dense woods. She zipped her jacket and wondered how long she'd have to babysit this crippled Brit.

It had been easy to leave the hospital. She convinced him that a further stay at the hospital wasn't really necessary, especially when she told him of the mounting hospital and doctor bills he was accumulating even with his meager insurance. And time away in her friend's cabin in the woods was just what he needed. Fresh air and just the two of them. Rog had checked himself out of the hospital and she had been the dutiful nurse, wheeling him to the exit and putting him in a cab. After her shift she had begun her pre-approved vacation as Sylvia Torrez. She and Rog met at his apartment in Hollywood as planned. She had tucked him into the back seat of her 1995 Nissan hatchback and they took off. All per Miquel's real plan to get the Brit out of town.

"Sylvia," Rog called from inside. "How bout a drink? Some of that tequila sounds good about now."

"Si, mi amor," said Sylvia, her voice not betraying the disdainful look on her face. She crushed out the cigarette. "Coming."

CHAPTER 30

Key elements of Johnny's world seemed to be collapsing in on top of him. Billy, his best friend and the lynchpin to his band, and his girl, Olivia, the group's drummer and siren for the male members of their audience, were so far apart they couldn't even see each other. And the more Billy pushed for a reconciliation, the more Olivia pushed him away. What this will do to the band was anyone's guess. Maybe I should start over as a solo artist, write songs for me and not a band, he thought to himself as he drove the Honda toward work the next day.

Then there was Rog. He disappeared right after asking me to check out those bikers. What was the leader's name? Del. With Smokey, who was at the club. Maybe they were involved in Rog being missing. But why? Even if the fight in front of the club was staged, they got what they wanted, which was to take over Rog's drug dealing there. And was this gang, SUR 13, somehow involved? Or maybe they weren't at all. Maybe that imposing guy across the street from Sylvia Lopez' house was just being a watchful neighbor.

The pieces kept shifting and adjusting in Johnny's mind, like a jigsaw puzzle with too few pieces to get a true image or pattern. It wasn't clear and precise, far from the mathematics of music, which was second nature to him. Once he began to play, whether it was an old song or something that floated into his head from his subconscious, it almost took on an automatic sequence, a progression that was simple yet complex, precise and refined.

It'd been that way ever since he got that first guitar from the pawn shop in Reseda back when he was just thirteen. It was a natural part of him from the beginning. Funny enough, although he was never a great student, once he began to play other aspects of his life began to show the positive effects of his playing. His grades improved, his confidence improved, even his ability to talk to girls improved. The only thing that didn't really improve was his relationship with his mother, Harriet. His father, Eugene, had died when he was twelve. The memory of coming home to an empty house, the ringing of the phone and his mother's tearful, strangled voice telling him words that Johnny considered the end of his childhood. And the beginning of a troubled adolescence.

Times had gotten tough for Johnny and his mother. Without the support of Eugene, Harriet was mostly out of the house, working multiple jobs just to pay the rent on the tiny apartment in Reseda that they had moved to. Johnny, left on his own, began to get into trouble, shoplifting, drinking, smoking and pill popping, cutting school. The only thing that had ever calmed him was music. The music that his father had made a part of his life. Johnny played his father's old CDs on a corroded ancient Walkman. If they had been vinyl, the grooves would have worn out. And when he found that guitar, he began another life altogether, a life rich and satisfying, a means of expressing his feelings, his desires and yearnings without the need of sitting in a shrink's office like his mother had forced him to do. It was liberating. And Johnny couldn't imagine life without it.

Maybe they could find another drummer if Olivia quit. Or maybe he and Billy could go back to playing as a duo. One thing he knew, he wasn't about to, couldn't stop. One way or another the music would continue.

He drove down the short ramp off Wilshire and parked in his spot marked "Security" by a sign in blue. In the next space to his right was usually Gene Murphy's gray Prius, which was missing today. Probably a sick day for Gene, thought Johnny. Wonder if the agency will send in a sub. He positioned his hat squarely on his head, the wide brim nearly touching the rear view mirror and exited the car, walking toward the elevator to the main floor.

After punching in, Johnny took his position by the front door. Everyone bustled about, the tellers behind the plexiglass counting the money in their tills, the loan and customer service staff and executives straightening paperwork on their desks, all preparing for the start of business. Another boring day.

After five minutes had passed, a man wearing a security uniform like Johnny's walked onto the floor, stationing himself across the doorway from Johnny. He was 5' 9', maybe 180, thought Johnny. He had dark features and black hair stuck out from under his hat.

"Hey man," said Johnny in greeting. "You subbing for the day?"

He looked over unsmiling at Johnny. "That's right." He looked away from Johnny and back to the floor.

"Cool," said Johnny. "I'm Watson. Call me Johnny."

"Right," came the reply. "Gonzalez."

He clearly didn't want to engage, thought Johnny. Oh well, he could deal with him for a day. Johnny was already looking forward to this evening. He and Shirlee had plans, their splurge, a once a month dinner out, tonight at Fabrocini's. He could almost taste the meatballs and spaghetti.

CHAPTER 31

By two that afternoon Johnny was entering his not uncommon state of restless boredom. The day had passed uneventfully, greeting customers that first said "hello," "good morning" or "good afternoon" to him, making his usual circuit around the floor of the bank once an hour, sitting in the break room for his fifteen minute morning break and for his one hour lunch break during which he unenthusiastically ate a ham and cheese sandwich out of one of the dispensing machines.

Gonzalez was no help. He hadn't said five words to Johnny so far. Not like Gene who was always happy, maybe too eager, to regale Johnny with tales of his life as an extra in TV and the movies. He had been a storm trooper in a *Star Wars* film, a prisoner in *The Shawshank Redemption*, a comatose body in the first *Matrix*, a soldier in Viet Nam in *Forrest Gump*. He even claimed to have played basketball with Michael Jordan while the basketball great was shooting *Space Jam*, although the thought of Gene, 5' 8" and portly to be kind, hooping with M.J. was enough of a stretch to make Johnny think that most of Gene's claims were at best an exaggeration or maybe even outright fiction. But he did keep Johnny entertained.

Gonzalez on the other hand was anything but gregarious. He dutifully stood at his post and made his rounds. But he had not only not said much of anything to Johnny, he had hardly said anything to anyone. Greetings to him from customers were met with a nod, maybe a grunt. Exchanges with bank employees were met with icy stares and an occasional "Okay." Johnny hoped that Gene was back at his station tomorrow.

"Watson. Gonzalez. Brinks." Dennis Solomon, the sandy haired manager of the branch with a vice president title strode past them. Johnny realized it must be Thursday and time for the weekly money delivery. Johnny followed behind Solomon, Gonzalez behind him as they exited the building and took up positions on the sidewalk. The armored Brinks truck came lumbering down Wilshire and double parked in front of the bank.

A gray uniformed man jumped out of the passenger side of the truck, leaving the driver behind the wheel. He banged twice on the rear door of the truck, which was opened from the inside by another uniformed guard. They each reached into the truck and carried out thick burlap bags, full of money. Johnny stood at the rear of the truck, Gonzalez by the front.

With a screech of tires, a gold Ford Mustang came wheeling around the corner, cutting off traffic and angling in diagonally by the back of the truck. The Brinks guards and Johnny froze for a second as if they were in a nightmare. Three figures, all wearing ski masks, bolted out of the Mustang brandishing sawed off shotguns aimed in the direction of Johnny and the Brinks guards.

"Drop the bags! Hands up!" one of the ski masked figures shouted in a deep, baritone voice. Another one of the masked figures ran to the front of the truck and pointed his shotgun at the driver, who lifted his hands up in surrender.

The money bags hit the sidewalk. Johnny and the Brinks guards all raised their hands. But as the almost incomprehensible action swirled around him, to Johnny everything seemed to be going in slow motion. He saw one of the masked figures in front of him look at the other masked figure, getting a nod in return and pivot his shotgun level at Johnny. He pulled the trigger.

"Boom!" Johnny felt himself flying through the air, landing on his side on the sidewalk. The ear-splitting explosion from the shotgun erupted a microsecond before the bank window behind Johnny shattered into a million pieces. Johnny was prone, Gonzalez on his hands and knees next to him.

As quickly as they had appeared, the masked figures grabbed the bags of money and jumped into the still running Mustang. The car backed up in a squeal of tires, smashed into the front grill of a red Mercedes SL stopped in the street, straightened and zoomed down Wilshire. Johnny watched from the ground as the car made a screeching turn south and disappeared from sight.

"You okay?" Gonzalez was on his feet, reaching down to offer Johnny a hand. He grabbed it and was yanked to his feet.

"Yeah. Thanks," said Johnny, looking at Gonzalez as if for the first time, reevaluating him and his opinion of the man. "What happ…how did you do that?"

Gonzalez brushed dirt from his pants. "I saw that asshole aim that shotgun at you and I reacted. Good thing you're not a bigger cat. You're pretty easy to knock over. Otherwise we would have both been shredded by that blast."

It was more than Gonzalez had said all day. "Jesus! That was fuckin amazing."

"Is everyone all right?" Solomon asked, a dazed look on his face.

A crowd emerged from the bank, mingling with passerbys on the street. Two Beverly Hills Police Department patrol cars pulled in beside the Brinks truck. A third car pulled up, a gray Dodge Charger, and two men in suits emerged. They spoke to one of the uniformed cops who began to cordon off the scene with yellow tape. One of the plain clothes cops walked toward Gonzalez, Johnny and Solomon, but Gonzalez motioned for him to talk away from the others. Johnny saw him reach into his pocket and show something to the cop, who nodded, said a few words and walked away. Gonzalez returned to Johnny and Solomon.

"The cops will take statements from you guys later," said Gonzalez.

"Okay," said Solomon. "I better shut the doors and report this to headquarters." He walked into the bank, avoiding the glass covering the ground.

"It was no coincidence that you were here today, huh Gonzalez?" said Johnny. "Or should I say Officer Gonzalez?"

Gonzalez smiled. "Actually it's Detective Gonzalez, BHPD. You have a good friend in the LAPD, Watson."

"Lapidus."

"Yeah. She called and asked me to look after you as a favor to her. Lucky for you. I even saw that meltdown of your band the other night. Too bad. You guys are pretty solid."

Johnny laughed. It lifted a weight of adrenaline, anxiety and shock off his chest. "So Lapidus did take the disappearance of Rog seriously," he said, more to himself than to Gonzalez.

"She must have. Especially after you told her about the cat with the SUR 13 tattoo."

CONFLICT IN THE CLUB

A phone rang. Gonzalez retrieved his phone from his pants pocket and answered.

"You must have heard, Detective," said Gonzalez, not bothering with niceties. "Yeah, he's fine. Maybe just a few scrapes from sliding on the sidewalk…Right." He handed the phone to Johnny.

"Hello?"

"Watson, you better head home. Come to the Hollywood station tomorrow morning at 10. And it wouldn't be a bad idea for you and your girl to stay somewhere else for a little while."

"Okay, Detective. And thanks." Johnny handed the phone back to Gonzalez.

Solomon reappeared and told them that the bank would be closed until Monday. He rushed off to call for an emergency window repair.

"You can head out, Watson," said Gonzalez. "If I need anything from you I'll get it tomorrow in Hollywood."

"Okay." They shook hands. Johnny walked down the ramp to his car, started the engine and drove away, the melee on the street in his rearview mirror.

CHAPTER 32

"You know you didn't have to come along," Johnny said, as he drove up the ramp onto the southbound freeway.

"You've said that a dozen times already this morning," said Shirlee. "And I've told you a dozen times that I want to hear what the cops have to say. I need to know exactly what's going on here."

"I'd like to know too," muttered Johnny, barely audible but loud enough for Shirlee to hear. She squeezed his arm.

He quickly looked over at her as he changed lanes, transitioning onto the freeway going east into Hollywood. She was wearing jeans and a tee shirt, same as him, with a pink Dodgers baseball cap pulled down over her forehead, hiding her dyed black pixie-cut hair. After Johnny had gotten home last night and told her what had happened, they had argued about the right thing to do. Shirlee initially wanted to pack their bags and leave town. But Johnny had told her of Lapidus' request for him to be in Hollywood the next morning. So instead of an impromptu trip north to Pismo Beach, they had spent the night in the Aces Motel on Sepulveda Boulevard. It was the only motel in the neighborhood that Yelp rated as at least clean and that Johnny and Shirlee observed didn't have men and women going in and out on short term stays in their brief, ten-minute stakeout before checking in. It was an area well-known for drugs and prostitution, but they had to find a quick place to stay the night before. They'd worry about tonight later.

Shirlee's phone rang, the chiming emitted from the speakers in the Honda, connected via Bluetooth.

"Hello?" she answered.

"Shirlee," a male voice answered. "I'm so glad I got ahold of you."

"Charles? Is that you?" asked Johnny.

"Johnny. Hi. Hi. Yes. It's me," Charles replied. "Are you in your car?"

"Yes, Charles," answered Shirlee. "What's going on?"

"I had another dream," said Charles. "You wouldn't believe it." Johnny and Shirlee exchanged glances, confirming Charles' statement. "There was a girl with long blond hair, but I couldn't see her face. She was standing in the middle of these big boulders one minute and all of sudden she disappeared. Just vanished."

"Okay," said Johnny. "So?"

"It was Olivia," said Charles. "I don't know how I knew, but I'm sure it was her. Is she all right? Have you spoken to her?"

"We spoke last night," said Shirlee. "She was fine. Excited about the new job…"

"I'm afraid for her," interrupted Charles. "Make sure she's okay. Okay? Will you?"

"We will," said Johnny. "We'll call her later."

"No! Now!" insisted Charles.

"Charles," said Shirlee, her tone sympathetic and reassuring. "We'll call her. Don't worry. But we've gotta go now. Okay? G'bye Charles." She disconnected. "Charles and his dreams," she said to Johnny, shaking her head in wonder and disbelief.

"Yeah," agreed Johnny, shifting lanes to the right in the morning rush hour traffic.

They exited the freeway at Cahuenga Boulevard. Johnny made a right at the bottom of the off ramp, angled right by the dry cleaners on Franklin and drove past Hollywood Boulevard. He found a parking spot on the street a block past the police station and they walked back toward the building.

"Hi," Johnny said to the sergeant at the front desk. "Remember me?"

"Should I?" said the Sergeant, looking down at Johnny and Shirlee with practiced nonchalance.

"I guess not," said Johnny. "Detective Lapidus, please."

"Wait here," indicating the wooden bench along the nearby wall. The Sergeant punched in a number on the desk phone, said a few words, nodded and hung up. "Down the hall to the left," he said to Johnny, pointing the way.

"Thanks," said Johnny. They retraced Johnny's steps from last week, turning left at the end of the hall and coming face to face with a tall black man in a three-piece blue suit.

"Johnny Whoops," he said in greeting, using Johnny's rock 'n' roll stage name.

"Detective Perry," answered Johnny, shaking his hand. "You remember Shirlee."

"Of course," Perry said, taking her hand. "How are you guys? A little excitement yesterday, huh John?" Johnny shook his head ruefully. "We're in here." Perry opened the door to an office at the back of the room, the word "Commander" on a plaque screwed into the door.

"Johnny," said Lapidus, standing in front of a desk. Next to her was Gonzalez, dressed in jeans, a black shirt and a Beverly Hills police windbreaker. On the other side of Lapidus was a tall woman in her thirties whom Johnny didn't recognize, wearing a beige pants suit. Behind the desk sat a middle-aged oval faced white man with four silver stripes on his police uniform. "I see you brought your better half. She really didn't have to come."

"Why does everyone keep saying that?" answered Shirlee. "After what happened yesterday, I'm not gonna sit in the dark like some mushroom."

The man behind the desk smiled. "I'm Commander Ashford," he said. "I wanted to see everyone involved in this task force and make sure the assignments were clear. Mr. Watson, thank you for being here. Detective Lapidus and BHPD Detective Gonzalez briefed me on what occurred yesterday. I'm allowing you here as a courtesy, Mr. Watson, since you are not a police officer. It appears, however, you are intimately involved in these investigations. Young lady, you must be Ms. Shore." Shirlee nodded her confirmation. "Again, we won't ask you to wait outside, but you must acknowledge that what we say here is confidential." Nods from Johnny and Shirlee. "Okay then. You both know Detective Perry. And this is Detective White," waving his hand toward the woman in the pants suit. "She's here on behalf of the West Hollywood Sheriffs." White nodded at Johnny. "Okay. Now that introductions are out of the way, Lapidus, you have the floor."

"Thank you, Commander," Lapidus began. "As you all know, we've had a number of separate incidents lately in our various jurisdictions that may actually be related. Mr. Watson's friend, Roger Cray, was a victim of a probable assault by the Death Playas bikers at the Whiskey in West Hollywood, although Cray did not press charges. A few days later Cray disappeared from both his hospital room at Cedars Sinai and his apartment around the corner here on Fountain. Evidence gathered about Mr. Cray led Johnny to a house in East L.A. of a woman named Sylvia Lopez, who we've looked into. She has an arrest and conviction record for prostitution and drug dealing and did eighteen months in Corona. Mr. Watson was questioned while at Lopez' house by a Hispanic man with tattoos on his arm of the street gang Sureños 13. I know none of you need a primer on those sociopaths. And finally, yesterday Mr. Watson was in the middle of a bank robbery at his work in Beverly Hills during which Detective Gonzalez, undercover at our request, saved his life. Anyone have anything to add?"

"Only that it was my impression," said Gonzalez, "that the attempt on Watson's life was intentional. Johnny did nothing to provoke them and the shooter deliberately turned his gun on him."

"Right," said Lapidus. "Thank you, Detective. It is my opinion that these incidents are part of a larger pattern. But what it means or why it's all happening is not clear. And that's why we're all here this morning. As these incidents have happened in West Hollywood, L.A. and Beverly Hills, we need to work this cooperatively. Your respective captains and commanders have all signed off. So these are your assignments. Detective White, go to the Whiskey. See if there are any Death Playas there and find out what they know. Detective Gonzalez, if you could work the bank robbery, see if there are any connections there besides Watson being in the middle of things. Detective Perry and I will go back to Lopez' house, have a chat with her neighbor. Okay?"

"What about me?" asked Johnny. "I'm not going to sit this out by the beach."

"That's exactly what you should do, Watson," said Ashford. "You're a civilian. Let the professionals handle this."

"That's right, Johnny," added Lapidus. "I suggest you take some vacation time from work and leave town until we get to the bottom of this. All right, everyone. Let's get to work."

The meeting broke with conversations erupting on all sides. Soon the room had emptied except for Ashford still sitting behind his desk. Johnny and Shirlee exited the station, accompanied by Gonzalez and White.

"Let me come with you to the Whiskey at least," Johnny said to White. "I'll stay away from the bikers but I could talk to Les, the new manager of the place." Shirlee's phone rang and she turned aside to answer.

"Look, Johnny," interjected Gonzalez. "We can't force you to stay away. But Lapidus is right. Take a break." They all exited the station together. "I promise if we find out anything about your friend, I'll let you know." Both White and Gonzalez rounded the building to the parking lot.

"Who was on the phone?" asked Johnny as Shirlee joined him, walking together toward his car.

"Charles again. Asking me if I spoke to Livie. I guess I'll call her."

CHAPTER 33

"Hi. This is Olivia Feldon. Please leave me a message and I'll call you back as soon as I can. Beeeeep!"

"Liv, it's Shirlee. Umm, just calling to make sure you're okay. Call when you can." Shirlee looked at Johnny, concern showing on her face.

"I'm sure she's fine," Johnny assured her. "You know, she's probably in a meeting at work and can't pick up her phone. You don't really think Charles' premonitions mean anything, do you?"

"No, Not really. But you have to admit it's eerie that he comes around with these warnings and all of a sudden things start happening."

"Coincidence. That's all." They were standing by the Honda and Johnny was hesitating before opening the doors. "You have work today?"

"Yeah," said Shirlee. "Why don't you drop me off at Norm's? Pick me up around midnight and we'll take a drive somewhere, stay for the weekend."

"Okay," said Johnny, opening the car door and sliding into the driver's seat, Shirlee climbing in next to him. They drove past Hollywood Boulevard, connected to the freeway, went up and down the Cahuenga Pass into the valley.

Twenty minutes later, Shirlee's phone rang as she was entering the restaurant to begin her shift.

"Hey Livie," she answered, recognizing the phone number. "How are you?"

"Hi Shirl," Olivia said. "Sorry I didn't pick up the phone earlier. Billy's been calling me non-stop. When the phone rang I ignored it, figuring it was him again. I thought you told him to give me some space?"

"That's Billy. You know how he is. Is everything else okay?"

"It's fine. Getting up to speed at the job. Why? Did Charles have another dream?"

"How'd you know? Maybe you're psychic too."

"Oh no. Shirl, I'll speak to you later. It's Billy again. I'm gonna speak to him." The line went dead.

Shirlee hoped the exchange between the two of them wasn't too combative. But she had no confidence in that outcome.

At the same time, Johnny was entering the Active store in Sherman Oaks. He found Billy in the back of the store talking on the phone.

"Really, baby…Okay I won't…No…I am…Just for coffee…I promise…Great. Thanks, ba, er Livie." Billy put his phone in his pocket and saw Johnny approaching, threading his way between the circular racks of hanging flannel shirts and pants. "Hey, mahn. Whachu doin here? Need a tee shirt? Hat? Pair of jeans? I give you my employee discount."

"No thanks. Here to talk to you. Can you take a break?"

"Sure, let's get some coffee. Mike?" Billy called out to a guy with long brown hair and a wispy beard wearing a baseball cap behind the front desk/register. "Takin my fifteen." Mike nodded back, never taking his eyes off his phone. "Come on." Billy led the way out of the store.

Two doors to the right of the clothing store was a Peet's Coffee. They ordered, received their drinks and Billy moved toward the door to sit outside.

"Let's grab this table," said Johnny. He sat at a table in the far corner inside the shop, away from the other customers.

Billy sat in the metal chair and blew on his coffee. "So what's up?" he asked.

Johnny didn't know where to begin. So much had happened since they were eating burgers and pie after the dust up with those bikers at The Hungry One. But he began to tell Billy as much of the story as he could without divulging the details of the coordinated police operation. About Rog leaving the hospital and his empty and disheveled apartment. About his visit with Lapidus and his later visit to Sylvia Lopez' house and the encounter with a possible member of the Sureños 13 gang. And his nearly getting his head blown off yesterday.

"Holy shit, man, are you okay?" exclaimed Billy.

"Yeah, fine. But I need you to do me a favor. Really two. Me and Shirl are going out of town for a couple of days. When we get back can we stay at your place? Lapidus thinks I should lay low for a while."

"Of course. And?"

"Go back to the Whiskey. See what you can find out from Les about whatever it is he has going there. Can you do that?"

"No problem," said Billy, giving Johnny his broadest all confidence grin. He looked at the front of his phone. "Hell, time to get back." He stood and they exited the shop, stopping at the door to Active. They embraced, clasping hands.

"How are you doing?" asked Johnny. "With Olivia?"

Billy let out a deep breath. "Well, she's willing to have coffee with me later. So we'll see."

"Keep it together, man. Easy does it, right?"

"Yeah. Sure. That's my name, Billy Easy Bates, Mr. Chill."

"Right," said Johnny with a wry smile. "See ya Monday." Billy watched Johnny turn and walk down the street. He opened the door and resumed his spot at the back of the nearly empty store, thinking of what he could say to Olivia.

CHAPTER 34

Detective Gonzalez sat in the Beverly Hills station on Rexford Drive between Santa Monica Boulevard and Burton Way, less than a half mile from where the bank robbery had taken place. He was still wearing jeans and a tee shirt from the earlier meeting that morning and had placed his blue baseball jacket on the back of his chair. A cup of black coffee in a paper cup was nearby, the third since he had sat down a couple of hours before.

The station was across the street from City Hall and had the same Spanish Colonial Revival style of architecture. Compared to the relic of a station in Hollywood, the headquarters of the Beverly Hills police force was relatively new. Built in the late 1980's and occupied since 1990, it was well maintained, clean and well furnished. Each desk had a still-shiny surface top and an ergonomic chair. Pictures of past chiefs lined one wall, all the way back to a shot of Charles Blair in 1927, the year the department was formed as a municipal organization.

Gonzalez studied the eyewitness reports, Solomon's, Watson's, the other bank employees', bystanders as well as his own. As is so often the case, the descriptions of the perps were wildly divergent. The number of men involved ranged from a dozen to two. Gonzalez knew there were three. The height of the men was mostly over six three according to most of the witnesses, but Watson and Gonzalez both had reported they were between five eight and six feet. Only Gonzalez and Watson had identified the car as a gold or yellow Mustang, the other reports had a Tesla, a Prius, a Toyota, a Dodge Charger or a Mercedes. But everyone had seen the sawed-off shotgun.

Gonzalez had obtained a copy of the video recording from the cameras in front of the bank as well as the city cameras along Wilshire Boulevard in that vicinity. The license plate number on the perps' car was clearly visible, but when Gonzalez ran it through the city's database, the car had belonged to a teen-aged son of a resident of Beverly Hills who had reported it stolen the afternoon of the robbery. It had turned up this morning in an alley behind Charleville Boulevard in the residential area of the city behind Wilshire, not a mile from the bank. Nothing was found at the scene except the car, which was being worked by forensics in the garage downstairs. If they were lucky they'd get something to work with. If they were very lucky, they'd find prints that didn't match those of the kid owner.

Gonzalez watched the video from the front of the bank again on his computer screen. Was it a robbery or was it an attempted murder? Gonzalez vividly recalled seeing the shooter nod to his partner and level the gun at Watson seconds before firing. He watched the sequence again. It looked like a signal, like the shooter was getting the go sign from his accomplice. Was the attempted murder a means to eliminate a witness and possible obstruction to the robbery? Or was the robbery a diversion, although a profitable one, for an attempted murder of Watson? If so, thought Gonzalez, what waters was Watson fishing in? They knew that

Cray had been dealing drugs at The Whiskey and certainly someone had literally muscled him out in the fight that put him in the hospital. But how and why did that escalate to murder?

The desk phone rang and Gonzalez lifted it off its cradle. "Gonzalez."

"Detective, this is Barnes in forensics. We got something here for you. The car was wiped before being abandoned but there's a partial on the driver's side outside mirror. If it's not the owner's, you might have gotten lucky."

"Thanks, Barnes. See if you can flesh it out and we'll run it."

"Already did. On its way to you."

Moments later Gonzalez' computer beeped, signaling that he had a new message. He opened the attachment Barnes had sent him and isolated and copied the fingerprint. Opening the federal database, he inputted the print and waited, staring at the screen.

After a few minutes he realized he could be staring at his computer all day. He stood, picked up his coffee cup and walked to the small kitchen at the end of the room. He dumped the cold remains in the sink and poured another cup, looking down out the third story window. A beautiful Southern California day, Gonzalez thought. Blue skies, not a cloud in the sky. A perfect day for a hike. Or a drive along PCH, watching the waves rolling in. Not today unfortunately.

He walked back to his desk and glanced at the computer screen. Pay dirt. The scrolling had stopped on a match. Guillermo Perez, priors for armed robbery, drug dealing, did stints in Chino State Prison for 18 months and for three years. Member of Sureños 13. No known address.

He picked up the phone and dialed a number he had written on a yellow pad. The phone rang twice and a woman's voice answered.

"Lapidus."

"Detective. It's Gonzalez. Have you and Perry braced the Sureños guy yet?"

"Not yet. In the morning. Why?"

"I'd like to tag along. I got a hit on a print from the car used in the bank job. Guillermo Perez, a Sureños 13 guy. No address but I'd like to ask your guy about him."

"Okay. Good work," said Lapidus. "Be here by eight tomorrow. Bright and early."

"Yeah. The bird and the worm and all that stuff. See you then." Gonzalez punched the off button. He smiled. A loose end to pull on.

CHAPTER 35

Billy drove the Subaru SUV from the store in Sherman Oaks, destination Hollywood. His work day had ended as monotonously as it had begun. He hadn't sold one item all day. There were maybe ten customers drifting in and out of the store. Billy thought Mike had rung up a sale at one point in the early afternoon, but he wasn't sure. He hadn't seen anyone walk out with one of the store plastic bags. Maybe he had imagined that a human being would want any of the merchandise they had to sell. He did have some stuff from the store; a few tee shirts, a pair of shoes. But if it wasn't for his employee discount he could get the same items cheaper at Target. And the public knew it, generally avoiding the tired enterprise that the place was.

Spending eight hours a day looking at his phone and singing along to the 90's hits played over the store sound system was one way to earn a living, although barely. But it wasn't part of Billy's long term plan. Sooner or later, they'd get a break, Billy believed. Sooner or later, someone with clout, with muscle, with good ears and an eye for the future will hear them and see them and realize that they had the goods. Whether it was Conflict as now constituted or some other version of the band or just Billy and Johnny, he couldn't guess at this moment. Ever since meeting in middle school and realizing they had a strong mutual interest in music and particularly in rock music as opposed to pop, hip hop, rap, even reggae, the two friends had been playing music together in one combination or another. First as a duo and then as a band, Johnny and Billy formed the first Conflict in high school, recruiting the only drummer they knew, a black kid named Cecil in Johnny's P.E. class, and Robert, a beginning guitarist who they had convinced to play bass. By their own estimation, they stunk. Although Billy and Johnny were passable at that point as guitarists and Johnny always could sing well enough, Robert couldn't play the basic rhythm needed, constantly flying off into bass solo outer space with little relevance or attachment to whatever song they were playing. Cecil on the other hand had a great feel for his instrument, but should have been playing in a 50's bebop band. He was a born jazzer, more Tony Williams than John Bonham. Which worked great when they wanted to jam, but he was so enthused with his ability that he couldn't just lay in a groove. Funny enough, a few years later Cecil did find his calling and became one of the most sought-after jazz drummers in town.

Conflict #1, as Billy and Johnny call it now in retrospect, did play a few parties and a couple of high school dances but mostly played in the outside carport in Billy's parents' house. It wasn't a total waste, thought Billy. They did have some fun times at those performances. And having Olivia there made it all the more memorable, all the more exciting. No matter how awful the band sounded back then, she always was Billy's biggest cheerleader and supporter. Billy smiled at the thought.

After high school, Cecil left for Boston and the Berklee School of Music, Robert was left to finish high school and eventually relegated his playing to a sometimes hobby. Johnny and Billy formed Conflict #2. Answering an ad they had placed in Craigslist, Roberto Benitez/Batter Up Beans or "just call me Beans" as he announced on the first day they jammed, was the tenth drummer they auditioned and he stopped the process in its tracks. Quiet, often with a book or literary magazine or blog in his hands, he was clearly more of an introvert than Billy or Johnny. But when he sat down behind his drum kit, he laid it down. Rock solid and fluid, he was a perfect anchor for the evolving band. And when Frank, the young preternaturally gifted cousin of Olivia, appeared and asked to play bass for them, the band was complete.

That's the way it was for a few years until Beans was hired to back an older black blues guitarist from Long Beach, "Guitar" Freddie Smith, who was putting a band together to tour the U.S. and Europe. That was when the present Conflict, #3, was formed. It was the musical arrival of Olivia, the trained pianist who had never played drums before. She stepped right in, adding a dynamic to the band that was fantastic, both sonically and rhythmically. She was a natural, thought Billy. I just hope I haven't messed things up so badly that she leaves the band. And me. Not only didn't Billy want to go to Conflict #4, but he hoped he hadn't lost the only girlfriend he really ever had.

Well, maybe I can repair things tonight, thought Billy, as he exited the freeway on Vine Street and headed south past Hollywood, Sunset and Santa Monica Boulevards making left turns on Melrose and Larchmont Avenues. Only a few blocks from the Paramount studios lot, Larchmont was a popular area south of Hollywood for restaurants and shopping, including one of the only bookstores, independent or otherwise, still in existence in Los Angeles.

Billy, however, wasn't looking for a book. He swiveled his head, looking to his right for open street parking among the diagonal spaces lining the curb and to his left, searching for an upscale coffee shop called "Sticks and Scones." The parking gods are with me, he thought. A black Lexus was backing out of a space into the street just as Billy approached. He pulled in and ran across the street, avoiding oncoming traffic and disobeying the "Cross at the Xwalk" sign.

There she was, as beautiful as the first day he saw her. Olivia was sitting at a wrought iron table under a green awning and in front of a window with the words "Sticks and Scones" stenciled in white. A cup of tea sat in front of her, the string hanging over the side.

"Hi Livie," said Billy, remembering her admonishment on the phone not to call her baby. Not yet, he hoped. He stood, waiting for her invitation to sit.

"Go get yourself something to drink," she said instead. She looked up at him, sipping from the paper cup, a neutral expression on her face.

"Sure, okay," said Billy. He opened the door, ordered and received a black coffee, added a generous helping of milk and sugar and returned outside to the table. He sat, blew on the hot drink and wondered what he should say. Olivia saved him from his swirling thoughts.

"Billy," she began. "What is the matter with you? What is in that crazy rasta mixed up brain of yours?"

"I…"

"No," Olivia continued. "Let me speak. For years you're telling me how much you love me, how you never want to be without me. And for the most part, you've shown me you do."

"I do, ba…Livie, you know I do."

"Then why the freak out when I thought I was pregnant?" said Olivia, her voice breaking as she held back tears. "All the years we've been together. And all the shit I've taken from my family for you. How could you act like such a dick?" The tears started to run. "Fuck, I promised myself I wouldn't cry." She fished a tissue out of her small purple purse and dabbed at her eyes.

Billy felt terrible and felt like crying himself. He looked up and saw what seemed like a swarm of other customers' eyes all boring in on him.

"Livie, baby, I am so sorry. You know I can be a fuck-up. But I never wanted to mess us up. I, I don't know. I guess I was scared. I have a shitty job that hardly pays crap. We live in a skanky little apartment in the death valley of the valley, Reseda. The thought of having a kid when all I really have is a band…You know I can't give that up. But are we ever gonna make it? Am I ever gonna even earn enough to quit that ridiculous job? I, I…shit, Livie."

Without thinking, Billy put the coffee cup down, stood up and dropped to one knee. Olivia's hand covered her mouth.

"Olivia," said Billy. "I don't have a ring. I'll get one for you later. I can't live without you. Please marry me."

"Billy." The tears started to flow again. "Oh Billy. You don't have to do that. Really."

"No. I want to. Let's get married. We'll figure it out."

Olivia could hardly understand what was happening. She was so mad at Billy, convinced earlier that there was a good chance that they were finished. And now he was proposing. And she was seriously thinking that she wanted to say yes.

"Billy, come on sit down," she said.

"Will you marry me?" Billy asked, refusing to get off his knees.

"Okay," Olivia finally relented, a huge smile forming on her tear-stained face. "Okay. Yes."

Billy leaped up, hugged Olivia who was still sitting in the chair and knocked them both over, tumbling onto the sidewalk, chairs, table, coffee, tea, Oliva and Billy in a splattering heap. They both started laughing as they rolled to a sitting position on the hard concrete. They heard applause around them from the once judgmental and now supportive crowd. Billy got to his feet, reached down and helped Olivia up.

"I think I owe you a tea," he said.

Olivia laughed, shaking her head. "I've had enough tea. Let's celebrate."

"Yeah. Let's go to Dan Tana's, get a bottle of champagne and eat like kings."

"And queens." They embraced, Olivia still in wonder and shock, Billy on a high better than any he had ever experienced. "Let's take the Subaru. I'll leave my car at the studio. You can drive me in in the morning. If that's okay with you."

"Your wish is my command," said Billy.

"Oh, now you're my little genie."

Billy wiggled his nose, grasped her hand and together they ran across the street to his car. The watching patrolman smiled.

CHAPTER 36

Johnny and Shirlee decided that they'd rather spend a few days in isolation in the cool, clean, crisp air of the local mountains than in the quaint but overly crowded beach towns north of Los Angeles. Shirlee had also reminded Johnny that the last time they were in Pismo Beach, he had gotten into a fight with a local.

A year ago they had been in Pismo overnight as they made their way north to Monterey and had just finished eating fish and chips at a restaurant/stand that was open on one side to the boardwalk and the ocean. Strolling through the town full of tourist shops and bars, they came across an old bowling alley. They entered and saw six lanes, a counter behind which sat the usual assortment of shoes for rent, a couple of foosball tables and a crowd of people throughout. Johnny had asked the man behind the counter if a lane was open, but it was local league night and nothing would open for a half hour or more.

They had ordered beers and watched the action, thinking they'd wait it out, when a guy with long straggly hair, carrying a beer approached. The guy beelined to Shirlee with his back to Johnny and began to talk to her with exaggerated motions, the beer sloshing over the top of the stein. Shirlee cried out "Hey! Watch it," to which the guy responded "You bitch!" That was enough for Johnny, who stepped between them, took Shirlee by the arm and began to lead her to the exit. But one step in, Johnny felt a hand on his shoulder pulling him backwards. He turned and saw the beer stein swinging in an arc toward his head. He ducked under it and landed a solid right to the guy's solar plexus. The beer stein went skittering along the floor and the guy collapsed onto his knees, gasping for air. All eyes in the recreation center turned to look at Johnny, whose adrenaline level had risen and was in no mood for backing down. Luckily Shirlee pulled him out before any further altercation occurred.

So they decided to head east rather than west, taking the freeway past Pasadena, past the towns of Monrovia and West Covina, along a mostly straight and monotonous path for over an hour. To the left were the foothills of the San Gabriel Mountains, scenic at times, but too far in the distance to provide much of a view. To the right was town after interchangeable town, to Johnny without much to distinguish between them. As they went further east, past Ontario and finally Fontana, the scene was even bleaker, old factory towns on the edge of the desert. The breeze blowing in from the Mojave swept dust over the cars on the freeway, speeding on as fast as they could go on this open stretch of road.

Shirlee sipped on a straw in a can of Coke. She was still wearing her waitress uniform, which wasn't that unusual for her even outside of work hours. She hadn't wanted to waste time changing, figuring she'd do that when they reached their destination. She lit a joint which she had in her backpack, inhaled and blew the smoke out the window, the warm air and dirt circulating inside. She passed the joint to Johnny, who took a hit without taking his eyes off the dreary road.

Johnny's phone rang and Shirlee reached under the dashboard.

"Hi," she answered.

"Shirlee!" the voice yelled on the other end. "It's Billy! And Olivia!"

"Hi Shirl!!" came Olivia's voice exuberantly through the phone.

"Hey guys," said Shirlee, looking at Johnny with surprise and questions in her gaze. Last either of them knew, those two were on the verge of being finished. "What are ya doin'?"

"We're having steak and pasta at Dan Tana's," yelled Billy. "And champagne." Shirlee heard Billy taking a huge drink of the bubbling liquid.

"Wow," said Shirlee. "That's quite a splurge. You celebrating getting back together?"

"Yeah," Interjected Olivia. "Together…forever…," she sang.

"Forever," harmonized Billy.

"What?!" Shirlee didn't know what she was hearing.

"Yeah, baby," said Billy. "We be getting hitched. Man and wife-ish."

"Marry-o-la," said Olivia.

"Oh my god!" said Shirlee. She faced Johnny. "They're getting married!"

"What?!" said Johnny. "Put Billy on the phone." He took the phone from Shirlee. "Billy? That you?"

"Yeah, mahn. It be me."

"Is it true? You and Livie not only worked it out but you're getting married?"

"Yup. It's all happ'nin." Billy laughed.

CONFLICT IN THE CLUB

"Wow. That's great, brother. That's just really great. Congratulations." Johnny paused, a semi zooming past him doing eighty-five in the fast lane startling him, his thoughts rocketing back to why he and Shirlee were getting out of town. "Listen, Billy. Before you get too lit, can you guys go over to the Whiskey and have that talk with Les?"

"Sure, sure," said Billy. "I'll chat em up and then we'll have some drinks with Vibes there. Wait'll he hears the news."

"Good, good. And Billy, if you can, speak to Les without his biker goons hovering around, okay? The less they know, the better."

"Yeah. Got it, mahn."

"Okay. Congrats again. Speak soon."

"Sure ting. Bye." Billy disconnected and the sound of female laughter was cut off.

Johnny put the phone down. "Can you believe it?" he asked Shirlee, who was crying, soaking the joint still in her hand. Johnny smiled, reached out and squeezed Shirlee's thigh.

"It's amazing," she said, resting her head on his shoulder.

The miles passed and they turned north near San Bernadino. The brown scenery turned green as the car climbed into the national forest. They opened the windows and let the cool air blow in. The fantastic phone call had seemingly refreshed the world. All of a sudden everything turned positive in Johnny's mind. Billy and Olivia were back together. So the band was back together. Lapidus, Gonzalez and the rest of the task force were on the job. He felt sure that after a few days they'd be able to come back home, Rog would be found and this whole series of events would be a thing of the past.

He smiled as the winding mountain road went past a sign saying "Big Bear Forty Miles." A secluded cabin in the mountains with his girl for the weekend? What could be better?

CHAPTER 37

"How long, Patrón? This here gringo is wearing me down."

Sylvia sat outside, her back against the back wall of the cabin in Lake Arrowhead, talking on her cell phone. She had told Rog that she was taking a walk in the woods, but the cell reception faded dramatically once out of range of the Wi-Fi set up in the cabin. She couldn't make the phone call that Miguel had demanded at this time on Friday night while traipsing through the woods. Plus it was getting too dark to see where she was going. Instead she retreated to the house, staying out of view of the windows the Brit spent half his waking hours gazing out of. Sylvia didn't know what he thought he was going to see, but she certainly didn't want him to see her on the phone. As far as he knew, they were on an idyllic getaway, two new lovers, although one with limited mobility and capabilities due to his cast. Thank goodness, thought Sylvia. His sexual expectations were also limited.

"A few more days," answered Miguel on the phone. "I'm tying up loose ends here in L.A. I'll be up to take care of the gringo soon."

"Well, hurry up, will you? He's starting to give me the creeps. Plus he smells bad. Those damn sponge baths aren't helping."

"Listen, puta," Miguel said, his tone and volume rising, anger and authority dripping from his voice. "You take care of the business I need you to take care of. You like the free house I let you live in, yeah? The money I pay you every week?"

"Si, Patrón," she answered meekly, cowed by the implied threat.

"That's right. You do what's needed and things will be fine for you. Otherwise you'll be a faded middle-aged whore out on Whittier Boulevard."

"No…" Sylvia tried to answer, to calm Miguel down, but he had disconnected. Goddamn pendejo, she thought, putting away her phone. But she wasn't sure if she was mad at herself or at Miguel. Everything he had said was true. She just didn't like to hear it so starkly.

Miguel had taken her off the streets fifteen years ago, when she was a hungry teenager, walking the streets of East L.A. and downtown, newly arrived from Tijuana. First her father when she was eleven and then her mother when she was twelve had left her, each attempting to come to the States and promising to send for her soon. Sylvia never heard from either again. In the orphanage the authorities had sent her to, she quickly realized that the only currency she had was her pretty face and alluring body. She learned to trade sexual favors for whatever she needed, primarily additional food, clothing and blankets. After two years there and what to her mind were endless such encounters, she decided to cross the border herself. It took her five days, running from other illegal immigrants, hiding from the immigration patrols, both official and self-appointed, barely sleeping and walking until her threadbare shoes started to disintegrate. But she finally made it to Los Angeles. Her forced training at the orphanage provided her with a skill that enabled her to eke out enough money to pay for a room in a Main Street boarding house.

It was on those downtown streets that Miguel had found her. Although only around her age, he was already intimately involved with life on the streets. Sylvia became the first of his women and she benefited from his protection. Eventually he moved her to the house in East Los Angeles, where she had initially presided over Miguel's stable. To his surprise, she showed that she was a natural in handling money. Later, when Miguel's business dealings changed and expanded, she served as a front for his other business dealings in the house. He trusted her, to a point she surmised, and had provided her with false credentials that enabled the nursing agency to place her in the hospital to look after Rog.

But she knew that without Miguel, her prospects were bleak. She was an illegal in a day when I.C.E. was a constant threat for anyone originally from Mexico and Central America without papers. A temp job as a nurse was fine but sooner or later someone would realize her degree and her documentation were fakes. And though she was skilled at making people feel good, her actual nursing abilities were highly limited. A legitimate job was not realistic either. Not that she wanted to earn the minimum wages any such job would pay her. She knew she had to endure whatever Miguel asked of her. Babysitting a half broken down wey for a few more days wasn't really all that bad.

Sylvia crouched, staying below the windows, and scampered back into the surrounding woods, straightening behind a towering ponderosa pine. She circled through the woods, hearing an owl hooting high above and exited into the small clearing at the front of the cabin. She stepped onto the porch and Rog's voice called out from inside.

"Sylvie, honey, you back?"

"Si amor." She opened the front door, flashing the warmest smile she could muster.

Rog was in his wheelchair, looking out the small side window at the dark forest. The ignored television was on, the sound turned down, the canned laughter of a situation comedy barely audible.

"Hey, baby," Rog said turning to her. "How bout we head back to town tomorrow? These woods are starting to get to me."

"Oh no, mi amor," Sylvia said, Miguel's instructions echoing in her brain. "It's so nice here. Just a few more days. Okay?"

"I'm just so bored with this shite on TV. I can't take it."

"I know, I know. Let me get you a drink." Sylvia went to the kitchen area, poured some whiskey in a tall glass, filled it with water, and, hidden from Rog, extracted a pill from a plastic prescription jar in her pocket and dropped it into the drink. She stirred the drink with her finger as she brought it to him.

"Here you go," she said, handing the drink to him and sitting on his lap. Rog took a drink as she placed his hand on her breast. "Don't you think it's nice here?" she whispered into his ear.

CHAPTER 33

Detective Frances White walked up to the entrance, looked up at the sign proclaiming "Whiskey a Go Go" and realized she had never been inside the famous night club. She recalled many nights outside the club, starting years before when she and her then partner would emerge from their West Hollywood L.A. County Sheriff's patrol car and keep the rowdy, mostly drunk kids from partying into the middle of Sunset Boulevard, break up minor scuffles and occasionally arrest a drug dealer who had made himself too conspicuous. But never inside the club. The situation and need had never arisen.

She knew of its reputation, once the center of the live music scene in the city and now a relic of that scene, a mere shadow of its former self. But obviously things inside the place were not completely dead and ossified. Her appointment to the task force and assignment tonight was a testament to that.

She had dressed in casual clothes, blue jeans that hugged her long legs, a Clash tee shirt that her father had given her years before and that she had kept as a keepsake. Her long brown hair was pulled back into a ponytail. She was pushing forty but hoped that with the red lipstick and blue eye shadow, she passed for younger and would blend into the crowd.

Entering the darkened club, she stood just inside the doorway, taking a few minutes for her eyes to adjust. She soon realized she shouldn't have been concerned about fitting in. No one paid any attention to her and the crowd was mixed. A diverse crowd filled the dark room, kids barely out of their teens partying like this was their time, middle aged suburbanites probably here to support their progeny who were playing at the club and even some senior citizens, maybe reliving their youth.

White wandered through the club, skirting the dance floor where no one was dancing but a half dozen people were standing, staring up at the stage where a singer playing an acoustic guitar was backed by a bass player and drummer. White couldn't understand what he was singing, the level of the sound system distorting the words and music being played. She ducked behind a support pillar by the bar and inserted a pair of ear plugs as inconspicuously as possible.

"Don't be shy. I wear em every night." The shouted voice came from behind her. White turned and the bartender, a black guy in his thirties wearing a purple headband was smiling at her. "Yeah, unless you've already lost your top end, plugs are a must," he continued.

"Aw, you so weak, Vibes," yelled the younger blond haired guy sitting at the bar, his hair tied in dreadlocks. "We don need ear plugs, do we darling?"

"Oh, speak for yourself, baby," the beautiful long haired blond girl sitting next to him said. All three of them laughed.

"Offer you a drink?" the bartender said to White. The blond couple drank from glasses of champagne.

White joined them at the bar. "A beer please. Are we celebrating tonight?" she asked.

"Yes, ma'm," said the blond guy, hoisting his glass. "To our impending nuptuals!" The girl raised her glass, they drank and fell into an embrace.

"Well," said White. "Congratulations." She raised her beer in salute.

"I'm Vibes," said the bartender. "These lovely people are Billy and Olivia." The couple smiled and nodded at White.

"I'm, er, Fanny," White said, using an old family nickname that she hadn't permitted anyone to use in many years. She took a sip from the bottle of Pabst.

"Here to see one of the bands?" asked Vibes.

"No," said White. "I've lived in L.A. my whole life but never came here. I was driving around tonight, saw the marquee and thought 'Why not?' right?"

"Right," agreed Billy, holding Olivia tight around the waist. "Too bad you din't come when our band is playing. Put these wankers to shame."

"Put these kids to bed," agreed Olivia.

"Put those babies to sleep," said Vibes.

"Put those sheep out to pasture," joined in White. All four now laughed.

"He's not lyin," said Vibes as the laughter died down. "These guys have a tight, rockin band named 'Conflict'. You ever see them on that marquee outside, you should check em out."

The name "Conflict" reverberated in White's mind. Hadn't she read something about that band recently? Wasn't that kid Johnny in a band with that name? She didn't acknowledge knowing anything about the band, not wanting to have to concoct a story to explain that knowledge. And the less these people know of her the better.

"Hey," said Billy, standing. "That reminds me. Les told

me and Johnny he might give us a gig. You know where he's at, Vibes?"

"Last I saw Les…," said Vibes, "…he was hovering backstage, talking to one of the bands. Might find him there."

"Ja mahn, I be back," said Billy. "Wait here, baby, okay? Have another glass of bubbly." He turned and walked toward the staircase leading to the upper floor of the club.

"I'll have another beer, Vibes," said White. "And Olivia's drink is on me."

"Oh, thanks, Fanny," Olivia said.

Vibes poured another glassful of champagne from the green bottle under the bar into her glass, then retrieved another bottle of Pabst, opened it and placed it in front of White. Olivia and White toasted and both drank.

"How long have you worked here?" White asked Vibes, dabbing at her mouth.

"Oh, about five years I guess. Seems longer."

"Many changes in that time?" asked White, probing but trying to sound as innocent as possible.

"Not much 'til recently. Just not the same without Rog, right Livie?" Olivia smiled in response behind her upraised glass.

"Who's Rog?" asked White, knowing full well but hoping to draw out Vibes.

"The manager before Les. He got into a fight and was badly hurt. Haven't seen him since."

"And things have changed since Les took over?"

"Yeah. A lot more assholes around." Vibes pointed casually toward the back of the club where a group of big men stood around, drinking beers and talking.

"Huh," said White in response. "That's too bad." She took another drink of beer. "Hey, where's the ladies room?"

"Back there," said Vibes, indicating the same area where the men were standing. "Just watch yourself. Those guys generally aren't too pleasant, especially to attractive women."

White smiled. "Thanks for the advice. And the compliment," she said, standing up from the bar stool and picking up her slim, beige purse. "Save my seat?" she asked Olivia as she stepped toward the back of the club.

CHAPTER 39

Detective White threaded her way past the few people standing about, alternatively looking at the band on the stage and around to the surrounding crowd, seeking something of more interest. You'd think the place would be more crowded on a Friday night, White thought. I guess the air really has gone out of this balloon.

She walked toward the glowing "Ladies" sign in the back, but slowed as she approached a group of three large men, long hair, tattoos visible on their bare arms. Clearly bikers. She stood off to the side, trying to be nonchalant and inconspicuous, while she listened as best she could to their conversation.

"…better…deal…"

"…not here. Les…moron…"

"…better than…"

This was getting White nowhere. Being surreptitious wasn't going to cut it in a place with a decibel level equal to an airport runway. She thought of a different plan. She moved off the shadowed wall where she was standing and walked past the bikers toward the glowing sign. As she passed the last of the three men, she casually stuck her elbow out and knocked the beer bottle out of his hand, the beer splashing up and onto his shirt and pants, the bottle shattering on the floor.

"Shit. What the fuck, b...," the biker yelped, turning toward White.

"Oh, I am so sorry," interrupted White. She noticed the belt buckle with crossing pistols around the guy's waist and a "Death Playas" tattoo on his right bicep. "I'm so clumsy. Guess I've had too much." She giggled as if drunk. "Let me buy you another."

"Jesus," the biker said, wiping the dripping beer off the shirt pushed out by his extended belly. The other two bikers were laughing. "Shut the fuck up," he barked, which only made the others laugh harder.

"Come on," said White, tugging at his arm. He looked at this woman for the first time. Not bad, he thought. A little old, but pretty cute. And those legs. They could wrap around a man twice. He let her lead him to a small standing table by the wall.

"PBR?" White asked him. She stopped a passing waitress and asked for a couple of beers. "Really. I'm really sorry about spilling your beer. I'm Fanny." She extended her hand. He grasped it much gentler than she expected.

"Smokey," he said, letting go of her hand. "I ain't seen you here before. You a friend with someone playing tonight?"

"No. Just thought I'd stop in, see what the famous Whiskey was all about." The waitress returned with two opened bottles of Pabst and requested fourteen dollars. White gave her a twenty dollar bill and told her to keep the change. The waitress accepted the large tip without smiling and disappeared into the crowd.

White and Smokey clinked bottles and each took a drink, White a sip, Smokey half the bottle. He put the bottle on the table and smiled at her, a gold capped tooth reflecting the spotlight from the stage.

"So," he said. "How ya like it? Pretty cool, huh?"

"It is," agreed White. "You said you hadn't seen me here before. You come here all the time?"

"Oh yeah," said Smokey. "I sorta work here. Make sure things run smooth." He finished his beer. "Hey, let's go outside, get some air."

"Not yet, honey," said White, knowing where this was leading. "Hey, if you work here, you must know where I can get some downers."

"Downers, uppers, coke, smack, whatever you want, honey." Smokey stood, grabbed her hand and tried to pull her along. She stayed planted in her stool.

"Don't be so impatient, big boy." She took another sip of her beer. "Hey, my friend told me that some guy name Rog was the man to know here. Is he around?"

"Shit, bitch," said Smokey, losing patience with this tease. "We took care of him weeks ago. Messed him up good. You'll never see him around here again. Now, come on. I'll get you those downers."

White made a big show of looking at her watch.

"Oh, hell," she said. "I can't believe it's so late. I gotta go."

"What about those downers?" asked Smokey. "Best in town, guaranteed."

"Next time." White stood to leave. Smokey grabbed her around the waist, pulling her into him.

"You're with me," he whispered menacingly in her ear.

She swiftly kicked him in the left shin and followed that with a knee to the groin. Smokey doubled over, and vomited out the recently drank beer. White quickly walked away into a dense part of the crowd and headed for the exit.

At the same time, Billy was upstairs, looking for Les. He had knocked on the dressing room doors, not getting any response. Inside the first one was a group of young kids, dressed in their best punk rock clothes, circa 1983 Los Angeles.

"Get out wanka," one of them yelled at Billy as he stuck his head inside the room. Not seeing Les, he took the punk rocker's suggestion to heart.

Opening the door to the second dressing room, he first didn't see anyone. But he did hear something, murmuring and heavy breathing. Billy walked in a few steps and a girl's head and torso rose above the back of the torn leather couch, her bare breasts visible.

"What?" came a male voice from the couch. "Why'd ya stop?" His head peeked over the couch back and saw Billy. "Shit, man. Get out, willya?"

It seemed to be a universal request. One which, under the circumstance, Billy didn't think was unreasonable. He left the dressing room and went up the short staircase at the end of the hall leading to the office. He was about to knock when he heard loud voices.

"How much do you think I can do, anyway?" Billy was sure it was Les. "On a shitty night like this?"

"You'll do as much as I want you to do, pendejo," a voice with a Mexican accent said.

"But there's at most a hundred people here tonight. You're asking me to…"

"I know what I'm asking you to do. But it's not a request."

"Listen, Miguel," said Les. "I can't…"

"No, you listen. I arranged for you to become the manager of this place. If you can't take care of business I can replace you too."

"But I helped you get rid of Rog, remember?"

"Yeah, you tried. But left it to me to finish the job, didn't you? I don't want to hear any more excuses, you got it?"

"But…" Billy heard a loud slapping sound.

"Do your fuckin job," said Miguel. "Let's go." Billy heard the sounds of wooden chairs moving. They were leaving the office. Billy ran down the stairs, down the hall and back down onto the stage floor.

"Come on," he said to Olivia, still waiting at the bar with Vibes. "Time to go." He took her hand.

"Bye Vibes," Olivia called out over her shoulder as Billy led her toward the exit, carefully avoiding the bikers tending to one of their own by the wall.

"Bye love birds," said Vibes, waving at the two retreating figures. He took the bottles off the bar, drained them in the sink and threw them into the trash. I guess Fanny's not coming back either, he thought.

CHAPTER 40

Detective Rodrigo Gonzalez waited outside the parking lot at the Hollywood station at 7:45 the next morning. He had woken hours earlier, careful not to disturb his sleeping wife, Jennifer, in their two bedroom apartment south of Wilshire, off Robertson Boulevard. He made coffee, drank two cups black and ate two pieces of sourdough toast with Nutella before showering and dressing. He fixed his BHPD badge to his belt, fit his department issued Glock 22 snugly in his shoulder holster and put his favorite blue baseball-style jacket on. Too early, he realized. Only 6:30, at this hour it would only take a half hour to get to Hollywood. Not wanting to spend too much time waiting for Lapidus and Perry, Gonzalez decided to look over the file that he had put together the day before on Guillermo Perez, whose print was pulled from the stolen car.

Perez was 5' 10", 220, grew up in East L.A. and was placed in juvenile hall detention at 13. His affiliation with SUR 13 began either then or before, the presence of the gang ubiquitous in that part of the city. His known associates, of course, were everyone that was part of or affiliated with SUR 13. The file had a list of twenty names of prominent members of the gang.

Gonzalez knew the area on the other side of the L.A. River well. His parents had grown up in East L.A. and Gonzalez had been born there and spent the early years of his life in an apartment just off Whittier Boulevard. He had been too young to be involved or recruited by gangs but he still remembered the tough looking men killing time in front of the taco stand where his father worked. Hector Gonzalez had been a cook there and his machaca was a favorite in the neighborhood. That had led to an opportunity to work in the kitchen of a Mexican restaurant in North Hollywood and the family left for the San Fernando Valley. Rodrigo attended middle and high school in North Hollywood, a former bastion of middle class white kids but a diverse populace of whites and Hispanics when he got there. Many of the white families who could afford it sent their kids to private schools by that time and an influx of families like Gonzalez' made up the difference.

It was there that the idea of becoming a police officer had occured to him. A job fair in his junior year had a booth run by two L.A.P.D. officers. Gonzalez had been curious and paused to look over the brochures. He had been planning to go to community college, probably nearby Valley Community in the middle of the San Fernando Valley as it was an inexpensive means of continuing his education, but didn't know at that point what he would do after that. One of the officers in the booth saw him reading the brochure and began talking to him about a career in law enforcement. At the mention by young Gonzalez of attending college, the officer told him that if he was an LAPD officer, the force would help pay for his higher education.

After that, the idea grew in Gonzalez' mind. He took the entrance exam and weeks after graduating high school, he began training and education at the Los Angeles Police Academy in Elysian Park, down the road from Dodgers Stadium. After his training and five years on the force, he became aware of an opening with the Beverly Hills police department that was a step up in rank and pay with the additional lure of a path to detective. Plus the advertised opening specifically said that minorities were welcome to apply. Within a year he was an officer in Beverly Hills and a year after that had taken the sergeant exam, passed and became a detective.

Now Gonzalez stood outside the Hollywood LAPD station parking lot when a Honda Prius pulled up to the gate.

"Good morning, Detective," called Lapidus through the open driver's side window of the Prius. "Glad you could make it." Lapidus waved her parking card over the electronic post, the gate opened and she drove through. Gonzalez walked in before the gate closed.

Lapidus exited her car as a Ford Expedition SUV pulled into the parking lot, Detective Perry behind the wheel. He parked next to Lapidus' car.

"Here's our ride," she said to Gonzalez. She got in the front seat, Gonzalez behind. Perry backed out, turned around and exited the parking lot and headed north to Sunset.

"What's the plan?" asked Perry, turning right and down the ramp onto the Hollywood Freeway heading south.

"We'll go to the Lopez house first," said Lapidus, half turning to address Gonzalez at the same time. "If anyone is there they can answer some questions about Lopez' and possibly Cray's whereabouts."

"And if the guy from across the street pokes his head out?" asked Gonzalez.

"That's just what we want," said Perry.

"Right. We can brace him about his gang knowledge, especially recent history. Perry and I will handle the Lopez house unless there's trouble. But if the neighbor shows, you should join us," she said to Gonzalez.

The freeway was crowded as usual, bumper to bumper as always on a weekday. It took them forty-five minutes to cover the ten miles from Hollywood to the Atlantic Boulevard exit of the 10 Freeway. They turned onto La Verne Avenue and found the small white house with the address that was listed in the public records in Lopez' name. Lapidus and Perry exited and walked up the path to the front door. Lapidus knocked, waited a few minutes without getting a response, knocked again and then rang the doorbell twice. Nothing. She knocked again.

"Hello?" Lapidus said. "Anyone home?"

Perry looked through the window to the left of the door but the shades were drawn. Lapidus did the same at the window on the right but with the same results. Together they stepped off the porch and began to walk down the driveway, peering over the gate. Perry, being 6' 3", had a distinct advantage over 5' 4" Lapidus.

"See anything?" she asked.

"Cardboard boxes," answered Perez. "A mess of em. And a clothes line with women's clothes hanging."

"Hey," came a voice from behind them. "Wha you doin there?"

Lapidus and Perry turned to see a Hispanic, in his forties, heavy-set, tattoos on his bare arms. This is the guy Watson spoke to, thought Lapidus.

"Hello, sir," said Lapidus, walking with Perry back to the street toward the neighbor. "Detectives Lapidus and Perry, LAPD. Do you know if Ms. Lopez is around?"

"You too? What's so important about Lopez?"

"What do you mean, sir?" asked Lapidus, as innocent a tone to her question as she could manage.

"I mean, first some kid and now you cops askin bout her. Whad she do?"

"Sir, what's your name?" asked Perry.

"Hey, man. I ain't have t' tell you nothin."

"Something to hide, Mr. SUR 13?" said Gonzalez who came up behind the group of three standing in the driveway.

"Hey, I see. You bring in a vato cop to brace another vato, huh?"

"No one's bracing anyone here, sir," said Lapidus. "Just trying to get some information. Now what was your name?"

"Jesus," said Chuy, giving his formal given name. "Okay?"

"Jesus what?" asked Gonzalez.

"Jesus Chin," said Chuy, knowing he was not fooling anyone with the obvious fake name.

"Okay, Mr. Chin," said Perry. "Are you familiar with Ms. Lopez' whereabouts?"

"No, I don know where she's at. I'm not her minder."

"Seems to me you are," said Lapidus. "You reacted pretty quickly to us looking over her house."

"You know. Neighborhood Watch and all that. You never know these days. Bad people around."

"Right," said Gonzalez. "So how long have you been Sureños 13?"

"Wha? Hey man, that was years ago. Folly of youth, ya know. Not part of the game anymore."

"No?" said Gonzalez. "Maybe you know a guy by the name of Guillermo Perez? This guy." Gonzalez pulled a picture of Memo out of his jacket pocket and showed it to Chuy.

"No. No, man, I ain't never seen him. I don know no Guillermo Perez."

"You sure?" ask Perry, leaning in close to Chuy. "Maybe a trip downtown will loosen up your memory."

"Don be harassing me with your lousy LAPD tricks, man," said Chuy. "I know my rights and I di'nt do nothing except ask you why you snoopin round one of my neighbor's houses."

"As far as we know at the moment, Mr. Chin," said Gonzalez, emphasizing the bogus last name.

"Do you know what Ms. Lopez does for a living, Mr. Chin?" asked Lapidus.

"Naw. Hmm, I think she clean houses. Like all good Latinas do," Chuy replied.

"Sure," said Perry, shaking his head at the nonsense Jesus was spewing. "You sure you don't know a Guillermo Perez. Goes by the name of Memo?"

"I tol you. I don know the man. Are we done here?"

"For now," said Lapidus. "Here's my card. Give me a call if you think of something." She handed Chuy her business card and walked with Perry and Gonzalez back to the parked Ford, leaving Chuy behind still standing in the driveway.

"Yeah. I be sure to do dat," he called out as the cops opened the car doors. "Shit," he muttered.

"Nice to meet such upstanding citizens," said Perry. Gonzalez laughed.

"Yeah," agreed Lapidus. "What a lyin p.o.s." Her cell phone rang. "Hello?"

"Detective Lapidus? It's Billy Bates. Can we talk?"

CHAPTER 41

Miguel angled the chicken taco into his mouth and took a big, satisfying bite. Man, there's nothing like Chema's, he thought. And being left alone for a few minutes. Memo was sitting at a table ten feet away on the other side of the red painted concrete patio outside the taco stand. Kique was stationed in the Chevy, parked in the lot and within line of sight. It was good to be alone, but not too alone. There was too much at stake to take foolish chances, to make a thoughtless mistake that could blow everything sky high.

He angled the taco for another bite when his cell phone rang. Right on time, he thought.

"Hola, Paco," Miguel answered.

"Miguel. Como estás?" the male voice asked. They continued to speak in Spanish. "So, I understand your record company is having a few problems with employees? Have you fixed the situation?"

"You know," said Miguel. "Nothing that I'm not handling."

"Good, good. But are you handling it or is it handled? Because you understand that this new business of yours that your partners here have given you is too important to fail. You can't let some non-cooperating employees interfere. It would shake our confidence in you."

The threat couldn't have been clearer if Paco had sent him a death's head text.

"No, no," he replied. "Within a week it'll be all squared away and it'll be business as usual."

"Good. Glad to hear it. I'll speak to you next week then." The line went dead. Miguel looked at the phone in his hands while he absorbed the message of the call.

This was too good to fuck up, he thought. After everything he'd been through. This opportunity was too good to fuck up.

He had started to get his street education at eight years old. That's when his father, Big Miguel Reyes, leader of the East L.A. branch of Sureños 13, went down for manslaughter and armed robbery in what his Uncle Tio, Big Miguel's brother, always said was a set-up job. As Tio told him years later, a rival gang member had snitched Big Miguel out, but soon after paid the consequences.

Uncle Tio did what he could, coming by to bring his sister-in-law, Miguel Jr.'s mother, Maria, groceries once a week. But it was hardly enough to feed Miguel, his two sisters and older brother, Jorge. And the meager salary that his mother earned as a maid in the San Gabriel Valley for some Chinese people barely covered the rent on their two-room apartment. So, like his older brother, Miguel hit the streets, doing whatever was offered for cash. Jorge got him a job as a lookout for corner dealers. That evolved into a small corner of his own. He was smart and quick with his fists when necessary and never ran afoul of the cops. The local gang members took notice. By the time he was thirteen Little Miki had become Miguel and he was in the same gang that his father had ruled. More opportunities followed until his earning power, whether with women, drugs, or robberies, and his ruthlessness and abilities with a knife or a gun commanded the allegiance of the rest of the members. The ones who didn't fall in line were taken care of. And like his father before him, he ruled.

"Memo, Kique, come over here." Miguel waved them over. "Sit," he commanded as they approached. They pulled up metal chairs across the table from him.

"They're nervous in Juarez," he said. "We have a week to get everything in order or things will get bad for us."

"What do you mean, Patrón? Didn't we take fifty large from that bank?" asked Kique. "That should make them happy."

"Don't be an idiot," barked Miguel. "You think fifty thousand dollars means anything to Juarez? That's fuckin lunch money. And do I have to remind you again that the money was not even important. You let that meddling gringo security guard get away."

"He got lucky," Memo interrupted.

"Yeah, lucky," said Miguel. "Right. I did some research on this Watson kid. You know he must have gotten lucky last year too in helping bring down R.J. Jackson."

Memo and Kique exchanged looks. Everyone had heard of the fall of Mr. Big, who had a piece of almost every racket in town. It was all over the media a year ago.

"That's right," continued Miguel. "I need you to find this Watson kid. Pronto. Put out the word. Ten K for anyone who finds him." Both of his men bobbed their heads, acknowledging the necessity to do the job and quickly.

"The kid disappeared," said Memo. "Never went to a hospital. The bank is closed so he didn't go to work. And I went by his apartment in Panorama City. He's nowhere around."

"He's somewhere," said Miguel. "And it's very important

to our friends and our mutual business interests that we find him."

'But, Patrón, Juarez must be happy about the drug trade in the club, no?" asked Kique. "You have that Les on a short leash like a little mutt."

Miguel snorted in exasperation. "That pendejo? He couldn't find his dick in the morning. And that group of bikers? Bunch of amateurs. You know that's not why we took over that club. The amount of drugs they can sell for us there is minimal. It's not the eighties." He paused and looked up the street along Whittier Boulevard. A quiet Saturday, people walking, driving, talking on the street, taking care of errands. It almost looked like normal life. But to Miguel it all had a glaze over it. A disturbing threatening shimmer.

"What have you heard from Sylvia?" he asked Memo, snapping back to the problems at hand and possible solutions.

"Nothing. Still entertaining the crippled British guy."

Another problem. "Okay, you call her. Tell her to keep that guy fat and happy. We'll take him off her hands soon enough."

"Si, Patrón," said Memo. He stood and moved away from the table, cell phone in his hand.

"Now if we can just find that Watson kid," Miguel mused out loud. His cell phone rang. Miguel recognized the number. "Que pasa, Chuy?"

At the same time Johnny and Shirlee were digging in to a late country breakfast at a place actually named "Country Diner." Eggs, hash browns, bacon, pancakes, coffee. It was a feast for less than the cost of a breakfast of warmed-over breakfast sandwiches, pressed potato and awful coffee at McDonald's down in L.A. Johnny looked up from his plate, a mouthful of pancakes, smiling at Shirlee.

"How much do you love me?" Shirlee teased him.

"Hmmm, mm, mmm, mm" were the only sounds he was able to make.

"Uh, huh, I thought so," she said, taking a sip of coffee. "Oh, I slept so well last night. Must be the clean country air up here." She gazed out the window, the mountains rising above the lake that the restaurant sat next to. It was too late in the season for skiing, but motorboats were on the lake, people with fishing gear already heading back to dock after an early morning expedition. "We should go fishing."

"Is that what you did in Fresno when you were a kid, go fishing with your family?" Johnny asked.

"Yeah, I think we did. I vaguely remember my dad, my real dad and me sitting in a rowboat somewhere holding fishing poles. Huh. Maybe it was from a movie," she said, dismissing the memory.

"If you wanna. We've got at least a couple of days to kill before heading back." He finished the last of the pile of potatoes and pushed back from the table with a contented sigh.

"Maybe we should check in with Lapidus, see how things are going?"

"I told her we'd be out of touch for the weekend. Anyway, I don't want to put the battery back in my phone while we're here. Don't want the possibility of being traced."

"A little paranoid, maybe?"

"Hey, getting shot at once this week was enough for me. It's just a precaution. We can pick up a disposable if we need to call someone."

"I can't wait to talk with Livie. It's amazing, isn't it?"

"It is," agreed Johnny. "Billy's always good for a surprise."

CHAPTER 42

"Yeah, Billy," said Lapidus. "Hold on a minute." She stepped into the passenger seat of the Expedition, Detective Perry behind the wheel and Detective Gonzalez in the back seat. She attached the phone to the built-in holder, started the car and pressed the audio button on the dashboard.

"You there, Billy?" asked Lapidus.

"Yeah, I'm here," Billy replied, nervous excitement rippling through his voice.

"Good. I'm in the car with two Detectives, Perry, who you remember from last year and Detective Gonzalez from Beverly Hills P.D. They can hear you. What's going on?"

"Yeah. Well, er, Johnny asked me to go to the Whiskey last night to talk to Les while he was out of town. You know he's the new manager there. Right. So me and Livie were there and I went up to the office."

Perry turned to Lapidus. "Didn't you tell Watson to back off? And he sends his friend in there instead?" he said quietly but with frustration to the other two detectives.

"You know he's taking this personally," said Gonzalez, still too softly for Billy to hear.

"So did you speak to this Les character?" Lapidus asked Billy in a normal conversational tone.

"No. That's why I'm calling. I never entered the office because I heard loud voices inside. Someone with a Mexican accent was telling Les to do something there last night. And then they were talking about getting rid of Rog. It sounded like the guy was ordering Les around. He said that he was going to have to finish the job."

"If that's the case, it wasn't a simple fight that put Cray in the hospital," said Lapidus, thinking out loud.

"But where is Cray?" said Perry. "No one's heard from him for a week now."

"Wherever he is, he's in danger," said Gonzalez.

"Okay, Billy," said Lapidus. "Thanks for the tip."

"Yeah. Okay," said Billy. "Oh, and one more thing. Les called the guy Miguel."

"Miguel," repeated Lapidus. She looked over at Perry. "That's good. Thanks, Billy. This could be helpful. But do me a favor. Stay out of this. I promise you we're on it and we'll let you and Johnny know when things are wrapped up. Okay?"

"Yeah, okay," said Billy. The connection went dead as Billy hung up.

"Think he'll listen?" asked Perry dubiously.

"As much as his buddy Watson did is my guess," said Gonzalez.

Perry pulled off the curb and drove toward the freeway entrance, heading back to Hollywood. The three cops didn't see the pair of eyes focused on them from across the street.

"What was the name of the guy we just talked to? Jesus?" asked Lapidus. "You have that file with Sureños 13 members with you, Gonzalez? See if there's a Jesus listed."

"And a Miguel," said Perry. "Odds are good that that guy at the Whiskey is a prime member."

Gonzalez opened the manila file he had brought with

him from the Beverly Hills station and leafed through the paperwork.

"Let's see," he said. "Yeah, here's a Jesus. Parma, age 25. Too young. Another. Another. Huh, there's five listed here. Two with the gang name Chuy. One's the right age. Jesus "Chuy" Flores. Bingo, lives on La Verne."

"You mean his last name's not Chin?" asked Perry facetiously. "I coulda sworn he was Chinese."

"Guess not," said Gonzalez. He ran his finger down the list again. "Miguel…"

"Lapidus," said Perry urgently. "Check out that black Dodge fifty yards back." Lapidus and Gonzalez both turned to look. "They've been behind us since we got on the freeway."

As the words left Perry's mouth, the Dodge came up fast, switching lanes. It cut off three cars in the fast lane to the sound of screeching brakes and car horns and gained quickly on the Expedition on their left. Within seconds the passenger door of the Dodge was level with Perry's window. Perry quickly looked left to see a shotgun being raised and aimed at his head. He braked hard, throwing all three riders in the car forward but restrained by their seat belts. A blast from the shotgun exploded in front of the Ford SUV as the Dodge rocketed forward, the deadly spray barely missing them. Another screech of tires and the police van snapped forward as a car smashed into them from behind. The three cops all lurched forward in the seats again and the front airbags exploded in Lapidus' and Perry's faces. The Dodge sped off, switching lanes and disappearing in the mass flow of traffic.

"Everyone all right?" asked Perry after he was able to clear his face from the bag. He turned to check on Lapidus and Gonzalez, unconsciously grabbing his neck. Both detectives nodded, although neither said a word. Perry put the portable revolving emergency light on the car roof. Traffic behind them had mostly stopped, drivers seeing the accident and its aftermath. The car that had pounded into the Expedition had taken the worse of the collision, the Toyota Corolla mashed in half, the driver stuck behind an inflated airbag. Perry unbuckled his seatbelt, squirmed out of the airbag's suffocating embrace and slid out of the car, walking to the Toyota. He said a few words to the driver through the closed window and with some effort managed to pull open the driver's door, easing the middle aged Asian man out. They walked together and Perry sat him in the back seat of the Expedition, Gonzalez moving over. Traffic behind had stopped, the police bubble gum machine visible, and Perry edged the vehicle to the far right side of the freeway. He switched on his police radio and called in the shooting and accident, calling for an ambulance, tow trucks and police forensics.

Lapidus, Gonzalez and the Asian man exited the car, standing by the side of the freeway as cars began to drive past them, avoiding the demolished Toyota. Perry joined them.

"I guess we've stepped on some sensitive toes," he said.

Lapidus grimly smiled and nodded.

CHAPTER 43

The task force reconvened at the Hollywood station later that evening. Which simply meant that White joined them there as the other three detectives had spent the rest of the day at the scene of the incident, conferring with other officers and members of the forensic team and getting a ride from East L.A.

"I've asked for a quick turnaround on those shell casings we found on the freeway," said Lapidus. "My guess is it's no coincidence that a sawed-off shotgun was used at both the Beverly Hills bank job and this afternoon."

"There's no trace on the previous casings, but if they're identical, we at least know it's the same shooter," said Gonzalez.

"Even if it's not…" said Perry, "…the method is the same and that also says something. Same weapon or not, we probably have the same or related shooter. SUR 13."

"So they didn't want Watson looking into Cray and they didn't want us asking about Sylvia Lopez," said Lapidus. "They must have had a hand in his disappearance. Maybe in the original altercation at the club too. Detective White, did you get anywhere at the Whiskey last night?"

White shook her head. "No. All I got was a big, dumb bruiser trying to manhandle me. One of the Death Playas motorcycle club. But I did see Billy Bates and his girlfriend hightailing it out of the club soon after."

"He called me," said Lapidus. "Said he overheard some guy named Miguel muscling Les, the manager of the club. Gonzalez, did you check for active Sureños 13 members named Miguel?"

"There was only one viable candidate," said Gonzalez, opening the file and reading from a list. "Miguel Reyes, thirty-eight, charged ten years ago with attempted murder of a rival gang member but never went to trial when the eyewitness refused to testify. Probably brought into the gang by his older brother, Jorge Reyes, now doing five to ten in San Quentin on a third strike for aggravated assault and burglary."

Last known whereabouts?" asked Perry.

"Unknown," said Gonzalez, consulting his file. "Oh, but this is interesting. One of his previous addresses is 4240 La Verne in East L.A. Isn't that Sylvia Lopez' address?"

"It is," said Lapidus. "Whoever this Lopez is, she's obviously tied into the Sureños gang."

"Yeah," said Perry. "But where is she now?"

Lapidus' cell phone rang. "Lapidus," she answered and listened to the voice on the other end. "Okay Sturgis, thanks." She put the phone down and looked up at the other detectives. "Sturgis from forensics. He's confirmed that the shells were identical to the shells from the bank job. Fired from the same shotgun."

"So where does that lead us?" asked Perry. "No whereabouts of this Reyes or Guillermo Perez. No sightings of Cray or Lopez."

"All we have is the address on La Verne and the sighting of Reyes at the club," said Gonzalez.

"I'll circle back to the club," offered White. "Let's see if the manager fidgets and gives something up if I show him my badge."

"Good," said Lapidus. "I'd love to get inside that place on La Verne but the D.A. won't approve it without sufficient probable cause. We're not there yet. Gonzalez, keep digging. See if we can get closer to Reyes. And print out a photo of Reyes for me. Perry, you and I are going back to East L.A. and see if anyone knows him." She stood, adjourning the meeting. Gonzalez and White exited the room, Lapidus and Perry following behind.

"I'm not suggesting it, because it would obviously be illegal" said Perry to Lapidus, "…but if a civilian, like maybe our amateur detectives Watson and Bates, check out the house…" He left the conclusion unsaid.

"You know we told those boys to stay out of it," Lapidus reminded him. "Right?"

"I'm just sayin," said Perry, opening his hands, as if showing Lapidus the obvious.

"Let's take a ride," suggested Lapidus.

That night was cold for a city boy up in Big Bear and Johnny had on his well-worn leather jacket as he sat on the porch of the Lake Motel, outside the room he and Shirlee had rented for the weekend. A facility that had seen better days, the twelve room motel was off a side road near the lake. It was quiet except for the murmur of a TV that Shirlee was watching inside the room. Johnny gazed skyward, amazed at the number of stars he could see, away from the lights and smog of the big city, a three-hour drive and sixty-six hundred feet below. The sky was saturated with lights. Johnny wondered how Billy and Olivia were doing. He strummed on his Strat as he sat there, idly playing nothing specific and not caring that the unamplified strings didn't sound quite right. As long as the tuning was on, it was okay with him right now.

"Fishing," he sang as he strummed. "All day long I've been fishing. It's the start of spring. Haven't caught a thing. I hate fishin…" That probably won't fit in a Conflict set, a thought that made him smile. *Maybe I'll start a country band.*

"John, Johnny, look at this," called Shirlee through the screen door. Johnny entered the room, holding his guitar in one hand by the neck. Shirlee was pointing to the television. A Swedish crime show was playing, subtitles displaying on the bottom of the screen.

"What?" Johnny asked.

"The killer is on the run from the police and to make sure no one would find him, he destroyed his sim card from his phone." She looked up at him. "Should we do that?"

"They're just being dramatic," said Johnny, "You know TV shows."

"Can't we call Livie? We're leaving here tomorrow anyway."

"Yeah, I guess so." He did want to find out what, if anything, Billy had found out from Les. He got his phone and the loose battery out from his backpack, reinserted the battery and pressed the start button. After a few moments the phone lit up and beeped, an indication of a waiting message. He retrieved the message, the phone pressed to his ear.

"Whoops, mahn." It was unmistakenly Billy. Johnny pressed the speaker button and held the phone out so that Shirlee could hear. "Went to the Whiskey last night.

Couldn't get to Les, but some dude named Miguel was givin him the shakes, big time. This guy is giving the orders there. Okay. That's all I got though. See you when you're back. You can stay with me and Livie."

"Hi Johnny." Olivia's voice chimed in.

"Er, that was her," said Billy. "Okay. See ya, bro." The message ended.

"I guess things are fine," said Shirlee.

"Yeah." He took the battery out of the phone and stashed them in the backpack. "We'll see them by tomorrow night. Shove over."

Shirlee moved to the right on the couch as Johnny sat down next to her, both watching a cop speaking Swedish examining a dead body on the television screen.

CHAPTER 44

Johnny insisted on having breakfast again at the Country Diner. That huge plate of food was too alluring to his grumbling stomach for his mind to ignore. So by ten the next morning, he and Shirlee were throwing their clothes in the backpacks, looking under the bed for missing socks and tossing everything, including the Fender Stratocaster in its hard case, in the trunk of the Honda. It was a cool, yet brilliantly sunny day and Shirlee was wearing her heart-shaped "Lolita" sunglasses.

"All you need is a lollipop," said Johnny, getting behind the wheel. Shirlee slid in next to him, kissed him on the cheek and buckled her seat belt.

"Let's go, Nabokov," she said. One of their favorite recent pastimes was reading the book to each other late at night and the characters and plot of the famous novel had seeped into their conversations. "Where's your phone? Let's call them."

Johnny knew who she meant. Having anticipated the request, he had retrieved the phone and reinserted the battery before they loaded the bags into the car. He reached into his jacket pocket and handed the phone to Shirlee. She dialed Olivia's number and listened to the ringing on the other end.

"Johnny?" Olivia's voice answered, recognizing the number on the screen.

"No, Livie, it's me," said Shirlee. "Oh, honey, it's so good to hear your voice."

"Hi Shirl," said Olivia, excitedly. "It feels like years since we spoke. Oh my god, so much has happened."

"I know. I'm so happy for you guys."

"Can you believe it? I went from thinking I was never gonna see him again to being ready to spend my entire life with him. Crazy, right?"

"It is. Wonderful crazy."

"Tell her to put Billy on the phone," said Johnny, rolling the car around the curves on the mountain slopes to the lower elevations.

"Johnny wants to speak to Billy," obliged Shirlee. "I'll see you tonight." She handed the phone to Johnny.

"Hello?" he said.

"Hey mahn," said Billy. "Where you at? Still at the beach?"

"No, we detoured to the mountains instead. Should be home by tonight easy. I got your message. Any idea who this Miguel is?"

"No, maybe he's the new owner of the club. Whoever he is, he was laying the law down to Les. I could almost hear him shaking."

Miguel, thought Johnny. Could be one of the bikers at the club. But Del at the Hungry One seemed to be the man in charge of the Death Playas. At least he was the one giving orders. And the bikers at the Whiskey were listening to Les. Miguel didn't fit in the equation. Unless… Sur 13?

"And no sign of Rog there?" he asked.

"Naw. But Miguel talked about finishing the job."

"Shit," said Johnny. If the guy could make statements like that, he was someone not to mess with. "All right. Chill 'til we get home, okay? I'll tell Lapidus about Miguel."

"She already knows. I called her when I couldn't reach you yesterday."

"Okay. That's good." Maybe she'll be able to piece this together. Johnny pulled into the parking lot of the Country Diner. "Gotta go, Billy. See ya soon."

"Bye. Be cool." The line disconnected.

Shirlee and Johnny exited the car, entered the diner and ordered breakfast. He was not as hungry as he was an hour before, anxiety about Rog forming a knot in his stomach. They both ordered pancakes and coffee and ate, Shirlee talking about Billy and Olivia, Johnny mostly silent.

Forty minutes later they drove out of the parking lot and followed the road down the mountainside. Johnny turned on the radio, which only got terrestrial stations and up here only one. A local Big Bear station was playing "Hey Good Lookin'" by Buck Owens, not exactly a recent hit, thought Johnny. But not bad for the drive. Shirlee hummed along, looking at the passing foliage, thick woods and greenery covering both sides of the road and an occasional break in the woods for a quick glimpse of the valley far below. "On the Road Again" played next, which seemed all too appropriate.

A half hour later, Johnny realized the car was running low on gas. He contemplated waiting until they got off the mountain but when he saw a sign that read "Lake Arrowhead 5 Miles", he changed his mind. Better safe than sorry, he thought, not wanting to run out of gas in the middle of nowhere.

"I'm gonna stop for gas in a minute," he told Shirlee.

"Okay," she said. "I could use a cold drink."

The road twisted and turned until a sign greeted them with "Welcome to Lake Arrowhead, Elevation 5,174 Feet." Within a quarter of a mile, Johnny spotted a 76 gas station, which was located next to a small grocery store and a post office. He pulled alongside a gas pump and got out to fill the tank. Shirlee went to the grocery store.

"I'll get you a Coke," she called back at him. As she walked up the two wooden steps into the store, she passed a Latina with long brown hair coming out, barely avoiding bumping into her. "Scuse me," said Shirlee.

"That's all right, dear," said the woman, holding a bagful of groceries. The woman smiled and turned away, looking over to the gas station. Isn't that the Brit's friend from the hospital, she thought? What the hell's he doing here? He looked up and their eyes connected.

Johnny had watched Shirlee go into the grocery store and saw the woman looking at him. Isn't that Rog's nurse from the hospital, Nurse Torrez? She was walking toward him.

"Hello," she said. "Aren't you Rog's friend?"

"Er, yeah," said Johnny, putting the gas hose back into the pump. "I've been worried about him. Have you seen him?"

"Oh yes," she said. "We decided to take a little vacation. Let him recuperate someplace away from L.A. It's so beautiful here, right? We have a little cabin the other side of the lake. You should come. He'd love to see you."

"Okay," said Johnny. Shirlee joined them, a plastic bag containing small bags of chips and sodas in her arms. "This is the nurse that was caring for Rog," he said in answer to the curious look on Shirlee's face. "He's here in a nearby cabin."

"Si, just follow me," said Sylvia. "It's only ten minutes from here." She walked back toward the store, opened the door to her car, backed out and waited for Johnny to pull in behind her. They left the parking lot, driving onto a side road leading around the lake.

"Johnny!" said Shirlee, alarmed at this unexpected turn of events.

"I know." He dialed a number on his phone as he drove. It rang once and was answered.

"Lapidus. Is that you Watson?"

"Yeah, Detective. I think I've found Rog. In Lake Arrowhead. I ran into the nurse from the hospital, Torrez. We're going to their cabin now. On Route 22."

"Listen to me, Johnny," warned Lapidus. "Be careful. Torrez' real name is Sylvia Lopez. She's mixed up with some dangerous people. I'll be there in two hours. Keep your phone on."

"Yeah, okay. I will." Lapidus hung up. Johnny looked nervously at Shirlee and then toward Lopez in the car ahead of them. She was also on the phone.

"Si, the gringo from the hospital is here," she was saying.

"Keep him there," said Miguel. "We'll be there in a few hours. And take care of both of them. Just be cool, comprende?"

"Si, si," said Sylvia. Miguel disconnected.

CHAPTER 45

The two cars drove for about five miles, circling the crystal blue lake. The cloudless sky and noon sun reflected off the lake like a diamond, almost blinding in its brilliance.

At any other time, Johnny might have been entranced by such a glorious sight. But now his mind raced. Was Rog really here? Or was it a trap? If he was here, were they really alone, just Lopez and Rog, a romantic, recuperative getaway, or were some of her menacing friends here too? The more he thought about it, the more on edge he became.

"Listen, Shir," he began, "…I want you to…" His cell phone rang. "Hello?"

"Johnny? Johnny that you?" The voice was quivering with anxiety.

"Who is this?" he barked, his nerves already on edge.

"Johnny, it's Charles. I just saw you in a dream. There were dark, dark clouds overhead. And lightning. Like in an old horror movie. It was bad, man."

"I don't have time for this, Charles."

"You were confronted by some sort of monster. It was horrible. I couldn't see it cause it was too dark. Or it was invisible. I don't know. But it was bad, really, really bad."

Lopez' car came to a stop in front of a small cabin. Johnny parked alongside.

"Ok, Charles," he said. "I can't talk now." This nonsense on top of everything else?

"Be care…" Charles' words were cut off as Johnny pressed the off button. He turned to Shirlee. "If things look dicey in there, I want you to make a run for it." He handed her the key chain with the car key and his cell phone. "Take off and call Detective Lapidus."

"But John…"

"Baby, please." She stared at him, fear in her eyes, but finally shook her head yes.

"Okay, good." He opened the car door. "Let's see if Rog is really here."

They exited the car and joined Lopez, who was reaching into her car for the bag of groceries.

"You made it," she said, smiling at them, her mouth barely visible over the top of the bag. They walked together up the steps onto the porch and Lopez turned the doorknob. "Now be quiet. He might be sleeping." She slowly opened the door.

The front room was empty. The blankets on the couch had been overturned and were partially on the floor. The TV was on with no sound, talking heads in suits discussing something with intense sincerity. Dishes were piled up in and around the sink, visible within two feet of the entrance.

"He must be asleep in the bedroom," stage whispered Lopez. She placed the grocery bag on the counter by the kitchen area, elbowing away two dirty bowls. She nodded her head toward the closed door down the short hallway and Johnny and Shirlee followed her as she slowly opened the door.

If they're here to get me, this is it, thought Johnny.

The door slowly swung open and there was Rog, sprawled on top of the blankets of the bed, the cast still on, a Rolling Stones tee shirt covering his chest, half a pair of sweatpants over his good leg. Lopez smiled and shooed them out of the room.

"He gets so tired," she said, closing the door behind them. "Must be the mountain air. But is good for him." She led them back to the living room and shut the TV off.

"I'm glad to see he's okay," said Johnny. "The way he disappeared. We were worried about him." He didn't know whether he should get her talking and engage her or get out and watch the cabin from a distance. But he was curious about this entire set up. Maybe he could get some information from Lopez. And maybe some of it would be the truth.

"Who is 'we'?" asked Lopez, glancing at her watch quickly.

"Oh, you know," said Johnny. "Me and his other friends." He didn't want her to know about the missing person's report that had been filed with the LAPD.

"Oh, si," said Lopez. "Of course you were. I'm so sorry, but Rog just wanted to get out of town after that terrible accident at the club. You understand." She smiled at them again. It was the same smile, pretty, practiced and becoming plastic in Johnny's mind at this point. "How bout something to drink? Beer, tequila? How bout you, honey?" Lopez asked Shirlee.

"We really should go," said Johnny. "Let Rog know we were here." He turned to go.

"No, no," said Lopez. "You can't go. You just got here. Rog will be so upset he missed you. Please, stay for a little while. Here, I'll make you a drink." She turned her back to Johnny and reached into the cabinet for glasses.

"Excuse me," said Shirlee. "Where's the bathroom?"

"Oh, right across from the bedroom, dear," said Lopez, pointed down the hall.

"Some water will be fine," said Johnny. "A little too early in the day for booze."

"Oh, it's vacation time," said Lopez over her shoulder. Johnny could see her lifting and pouring the bottle of tequila and mixing in soda water.

Shirlee closed the door to the bathroom and took a deep breath. There was something about Lopez that gave her the creeps. The fake sincerity. The insistence that they stay. Even if no one but she and Rog were here. She opened the mirrored door to the medicine cabinet. Generic ibuprofen, large bandages, plastic prescription bottles. She picked one bottle up. Empty. The label read "Oxycodone." The other bottle was the same, but half full. That was an awfully strong pain killer, she thought. She put the bottle down, flushed the toilet and walked stealthily down the hall. Lopez was putting a pill into a drink, stirring it with a swizzle stick and handing it to Johnny. She turned to look at Shirlee, walking back to the kitchen.

"I have one for you too, chica."

Johnny raised the glass to his lips.

"Johnny! Don't!" yelled Shirlee. "Don't drink that. It's spiked."

Johnny stopped just as a few drops of liquid slid into his mouth. He spit it out, the droplets spraying the room.

"What the hell?" he said, taking a step toward Lopez. She turned quickly, opened a drawer and wheeled back, holding a small 22 caliber gun in her right hand, its barrel aimed at Johnny.

"Sit down," Lopez ordered, indicating the couch with a wave of the gun. Johnny and Shirlee backed up and sat, not taking their eyes off Lopez or the gun the entire time. "You could have made this so easy. So simple. Have a drink, get relaxed, have a little sleep, no problem. But no. So now we sit.""

She sat on a kitchen barstool, the gun still leveled at them. With her other hand she picked up the TV remote. She turned the sound up to a barely audible level and toggled through stations until she came to a local Univision station, showing a daytime soap opera. "We'll watch this. You gringos can learn a little Spanish while we wait."

"Wait for what?" asked Johnny, trying to calculate how long it would be before Lapidus arrived.

"You'll see," said Lopez.

CHAPTER 46

There was no way either Shirlee or Johnny were learning Spanish today, TV or no TV, except for pistola. Lopez continued to level the gun at them while she shifted her eyes back and forth, from the TV screen to them and back again. Like she was at a tennis match, between the insipid and the deadly. An hour passed. Maybe more. All sense of time had become distorted by the intensity and stress of a gun being pointed at them.

After a while, Johnny began to time her eye movements. Lopez was consistent, even during the commercials, which he recognized by sound because the Spanish station used the same trick as English language stations of pumping up the volume level to keep the audience's attention. He caught Shirlee's eye and looked downward. Lopez looked back and they both stared back at her. When Lopez looked away, Johnny motioned with his eyebrows, tilting them upward indicating they should move apart. Shirlee looked up and gave him a quick nod. The next time Lopez looked away, Johnny and Shirlee both moved apart from each other on the couch. A few inches of separation. A moment later, they did it again. And again. Finally they were almost a foot apart, too far, thought Johnny, to shoot them both before one of them reached her. Just in case things went bad. Or if he got the chance.

"Ha! Ha! Eso es divertido!" Lopez exclaimed, enjoying the show. Johnny braced himself, about to spring off the couch at the distracted Lopez. A voice called loudly from down the hall.

"Sylvia. Sylvia. Where are you? You watching that soap opera shite?" It was unmistakenly Rog's voice and Lopez' head whipped around, taking in first Shirlee, then Johnny. Johnny relaxed, sinking into the couch cushions.

"Si, amor," she said.

"Rog!" called out Johnny.

"Silencio!" demanded Lopez, aiming the gun at Johnny's head.

"Johnny? That you?" called Rog. "What the hell's going on out there?"

"Up, you two," said Lopez. "You want to see your friend? Let's go." She waved the gun, motioning Shirlee and Johnny up from the couch. They stood and filed in front of her, walking toward the hallway, Lopez trailing behind.

"Johnny," called Rog as he stepped into the bedroom. "You're his girl, right? Shirlee, right? What is this?" He stopped talking as Lopez walked into the room, still holding the 22.

"Oh, we're gonna have a little party," said Lopez. "Sit in those chairs. Put them next to the bed." She indicated the two thin wooden chairs by the wall. Johnny and Shirlee sat.

"Nice friends you have," said Johnny.

"What is this, Sylvia?" Rog asked.

"Don't worry about it," replied Lopez. "Aren't you comfortable? Maybe you want another drink. With another little fall asleep pill in it?"

"I knew it, you bitch," said Rog, throwing the covers off his legs and trying to move toward her, his cast clanking against his wheelchair.

"Take it easy," said Lopez, turning the gun on him. "I'd hate to have to shoot you. At least not until I get paid."

"Oh, no, please, don't!" cried Shirlee, her hand to her mouth, tears welling up in her eyes.

"How could you, ya bitch?!" said Rog.

"You'll never get away with this!" yelled Johnny.

Lopez' gun rotated from one to the other as each cried out again.

"Please don't."

"Ya lowly skank bitch!"

"They're comin for ya."

Lopez yelled, "Stop!" and fired a shot into the ceiling.

As soon as the gun was pointed upward, Johnny bolted from the chair. The shot nearly deafened him being so close to his ear as he rushed Lopez, grabbing her gun arm and twisting. Another shot rang out as Lopez clung tightly to the gun, the bullet smashing into the full length mirror hanging on the wall.

"Run, Shirlee! Get out," Johnny yelled. He smacked Lopez' hand against the bedframe, but she held on, howling like an angered beast.

Shirlee ran out of the room and through the house. The sounds of her hurried footfalls outside, the slamming of the car door and the start of the engine were clearly audible. The car tires screeched as she raced off.

Lopez scratched at Johnny's eyes as he twisted around to get a better grip on her gun hand. He involuntarily let go, a hand reaching up to his eyes.

"Ha," said Lopez, triumphantly, turning the gun on Johnny. She was on her knees, her elbows propped up by the mattress on the bed. "I don think we're gonna wait any longer. Oh!"

Rog smashed his bad leg, forty pounds of hard cast, on the back of Lopez' head. She seemed stunned for a second, immobile, then collapsed, her face into the mattress, the gun falling, bouncing to the floor.

Johnny scooped up the gun, putting it in his waistband and checked Lopez, who was unconscious. "You okay?" he asked Rog.

"Yeah, sure. Can't believe it. The skank. You know, she wasn't even that good a lay." Rog turned to Johnny. "Well, maybe she was. Shit. Here, use clothes there to tie her up."

Johnny picked up discarded tee shirts from the floor and tied Lopez' hands and feet. Moaning sounds rolled out of her.

"Where'd you send your girl?" asked Rog.

"She's getting away from here. She knows to call the cops. They're already on the way."

"You really are the detective, ain't cha?" said Rog.

The sound of a car approaching came through the window, but it didn't sound like the engine of the Honda to Johnny. He looked out the window and saw a brown Chevy.

"Now, we'll see," slurred Lopez. Johnny turned to see her smiling wickedly. "Hey M…" she began to yell. Rog stuffed a stray sock in her mouth, cutting her off.

Johnny watched out the window as three men exited the car, one of them holding a struggling Shirlee by the upper arm.

"Hey Gringo," called the one in the middle, standing fifty yards from the house. "You lose something? This little thing yours?"

"Johnny," Shirlee called out. "They ran me off the road."

"Let her go," said Johnny from behind the wall of the cabin.

"No, I think we'll just come in there." He took a step forward. A shot rang out from the house and the three men dived to the ground, dragging Shirlee down with them into the dirt. The bullet pinged off a tree behind them, the shot over their heads.

"Let her go or the next shot will be between your eyes," called Johnny.

The men on the ground all scrambled back behind the car, yanking Shirlee along. They drew 45s from their belts. The leader pulled the trigger and fired a shot toward the house, shattering a window.

"We got guns too," he yelled. "Now let Sylvia out."

Lopez spit the sock out and yelled "Miguel, Miguel!"

"Let the girl go and I'll let Sylvia go," said Johnny. He knew that they probably had him outgunned as well as outmanned. All he had was Lopez' 22 and there were only three shots left.

"I don think so," said Miguel. A fuselage of bullets erupted. Johnny yanked Rog off the bed onto the floor as windows, lamps, a dresser splintered and the mattress and pillows exploded in a cloud of feathers and dust. Johnny looked up from the floor and saw Lopez. Her head was turned to him and her eyes were open. Blood was pouring from her mouth and gaping bullet holes were visible on her back.

"You killed your own woman," yelled Johnny.

"That's too bad," called Miguel. "Now I'm gonna kill you and that Brit friend of yours." He signaled Memo, who emerged from behind the car and ran toward the front door of the cabin, Miguel and Kique firing covering shots toward the bedroom window.

Johnny scuttled on the floor out into the living room, covering his head from falling debris. He fired the 22 when

Memo opened the door. Memo's hand went to his throat. Blood spurted over his fingers as he dropped to his knees, then toppled over, falling backwards through the doorway.

"Aaagh!" cried Miguel. "I am gonna skin you alive before I kill you, gringo," he shouted. "But first I'm gonna kill your girlfriend while you watch." He pulled and flipped open an eight inch switchblade from his belt and reached down for Shirlee.

She wasn't there. In the chaos, while Miguel and Kique were firing as Memo rushed the house, she had crawled away from the car and, on hands and knees, slid into the cover of the forest.

"Where is the gringa?" yelled Miguel. "Go get her," he said to Kique, who ran toward the trees. Johnny fired a shot and Kique spun and hit the dirt, a bullet through his upper right side. "Damn it!" yelled Miguel. He popped up from behind the car, took two steps, then dived to the ground. A shot came from the house and flew three feet over his head. Miguel jumped up and ran to the woods.

Johnny knew he was out of ammunition. In a panic, he ran from the house toward the woods where Miguel had disappeared when the sound of sirens filled the air. Two matching Ford Crown Vics skidded next to the Chevy, their lights flashing. Four figures jumped out of the cars before the engines had died, Lapidus and Perry from the front car, White and Gonzalez from the rear.

"Find Shirlee," Johnny shouted at them as he raced into the woods.

"I'm here. Johnny, I'm here," Shirlee called from twenty yards away, emerging from the tree line. Johnny ran over and embraced her, tighter than he had ever held another human being. "It's okay, baby," she said. "I'm okay." They kissed.

"Their leader, some guy named Miguel, ran off into the woods," Johnny told Lapidus after they disentangled.

"Okay. You guys," Lapidus said to the other three detectives. "Search the woods. Be careful. I'll call in the locals and put out an APB." Lapidus went to the Ford and talked into the radio transmitter.

Perry saw Kique on the ground, blood oozing from his shoulder.

"Got a live one here," he called out to Lapidus. "Better get an ambulance." He slapped a pair of handcuffs on him, ripped a piece of Kique's shirt off and pressed it to the wound. "Hold this tight, hombre," he told Kique. "You'll live." He caught up with White and Gonzalez and the three detectives disappeared into the forest. Lapidus, Shirlee and Johnny returned to the cabin, now shredded by gunfire.

CHAPTER 47

"Goddamn it!" thought Miguel, furious and frustrated at the turn of events. All plans for finding the white girl who had run into the woods were abandoned. The sirens had fixed that. That kid must have tipped off the police. Now the only thing to do was run. Get as far away from this fucked up scene as possible. He heard the sounds of multiple sirens in the distance.

How could things get worse? Memo gone, Kique maybe also gone. Or at least in custody. Even Sylvia is gone. Who's gonna handle the other whores and who's gonna live in the transit house? That place on La Verne is too important. I've got to have someone there I can trust.

Miguel stumbled over a branch, brushed against a tree and righted himself. It was still light out, the sun not setting this time of year for another couple of hours, but the dense foliage overhead made it hard to see. The path sloped downhill.

Just get to a road, he thought. That would lead to civilization of some sort and then I can get out of this hellhole. Damn it! Thirty minutes ago everything was falling into place. Take out the kid and the Brit, the only real threats to me. Leave the cops holding their dicks. But now red lights and sirens are flashing everywhere. I've gotta get back to L.A.

He heard faint voices behind him and quickened his pace, running when he could, leaping over fallen tree limbs. He ran barely in control. His left foot caught between two hidden pieces of fallen wood covered by leaves and he tripped and fell, sprawling face first into the forest floor.

"Hey," he heard a shout from behind. "Did you hear that?" The cops had heard him fall. He scrambled to his feet and continued running. His ankle was aching, having been twisted by the fall.

"This way!" The voices were getting louder. Maybe one hundred yards away. He continued to thread between the trees and the fallen limbs, guided by the filtered sunlight. The dim dopplering sound of a car's engine broke through the woods. He was close to a road!

"He went this way." He heard the voices behind him, now much closer, maybe twenty-five yards. He could hear the footsteps of the cops crunching leaves underfoot as they hurried toward him. Where is that road?

"White, over here." They're too close. Miguel dove behind a large boulder, big enough for him to crouch down and hide. In front of him he could hear an occasional car approach and fade away. But behind him he could now see three cops, two men and a woman, in a slight clearing fifteen feet away, back in the direction he had just come.

"I hear the road," said the woman. "If he hasn't made it there yet, he's close." All three pulled their guns and walked slowly forward, spread out with ten feet between them.

Miguel quietly opened his switchblade, holding his hand over the opening blade and tensed. It was useless to get into a shoot-out with three cops here. He'd never leave alive. The Hispanic cop was nearest and walking toward the boulder. If he walked past, Miguel would grab him, cover his mouth and kill him, hopefully without alerting the others until he could pull his own gun. At least improve the odds.

Gonzalez took another step closer to the boulder and stopped, swiveling his head, straining to see any signs of the fleeing gang member. He peered over the top of the boulder. Nothing but trees as far as he could see. He stepped to his right, his hand on the big rock, using it for balance as he prepared to walk past it.

"Hey guys," called out Perry from twenty yards to Gonzalez' left. "There's the road. He must have found it and made his way to town."

Gonzalez turned away from the boulder and quickly walked toward Perry, unknowingly leaving Miguel, blade in hand, to take a deep breath. Hearing the retreating footsteps, Miguel peered around the boulder in time to see the three cops half running, half sliding down the hill and out of sight, presumably to the road below. He waited five minutes and then followed.

From the top of the hill, he could see the cops standing on the side of the road, not thirty feet away. They were talking but Miguel couldn't hear what they were saying. After a few minutes, a Crown Vic, obviously a cop car, came into view, made a u-turn and pulled up alongside the waiting cops. They opened the car doors, piled in and Miguel could see the female driver put the car in gear and drive off the way she came. Probably back to the cabin, he thought.

Miguel sat and wiggled his way down the hill to the road once the Crown Vic had disappeared from view. If they went that way, I'm going this way, he thought, walking in the opposite direction of the police car. He recalled passing a town maybe ten miles from the cabin, so he was maybe seven miles away from there.

A car approached and he stuck out his thumb. A middle-aged white man in a Toyota Tacoma truck zipped past him doing forty, not slowing. Miguel continued to walk. He'd gone a mile or more when another car approached. A beat up gray pickup truck, teenage boy at the wheel, a joint hanging from his mouth. He waved as he drove past Miguel. "Puto," he thought.

Night was starting to fall when he finally walked into the outskirts of the town of Lake Arrowhead. Four other cars had passed him as he walked but after the first two passing cars, he had decided it would be better to not attract any notice in this little burg, a guy filthy from the woods covered with tats barely concealed under his light jacket, hitching from the direction of a shoot-out. He could see from his vantage point on the road at the top of the ridge that shoppers and diners were out on the town streets, a quarter of a mile away. Cars were parked back to back along the side of the road.

Miguel picked out an old Dodge pickup, popped the door lock with his knife, stripped the ignition wires and started the car. He looked around, saw no one reacting and steered the car onto the road. "Los Angeles 80 Miles" read the sign as he passed the other side of the town. L.A. awaited as did some serious business.

CHAPTER 43

"No, Billy, we're fine. Everything's worked out." Johnny kept trying to reassure his friend, but Billy couldn't take it all in without a million questions and concerns. The conversation was already ten minutes in when Shirlee held out her hand, silently signaling Johnny to hand over the phone.

"Billy," she said. "We'll be home in a couple of hours. We can talk more then. Yes, I know we were supposed to get home yesterday but you know. There was questioning by waves of police. If it wasn't for Detective Lapidus, we might be in jail up here. Just tell Livie we'll see you guys soon, okay? Okay. Good. Bye." She handed the phone to Johnny.

"Bates okay?" asked Lapidus from the front seat, turning to face Shirlee and Johnny in the back of the Crown Vic.

"He'll be fine," said Shirlee. She looked out the window at the trees blurring past on the side of the mountain road as they drove down toward San Bernadino. It was midday on Monday.

After the crime scene had been roped off, Kique booked for the murder of Sylvia Lopez and statements taken from Johnny, Shirlee and Rog, Lapidus had authorized motel rooms in town for everyone rather than drive the mountain roads late the previous night. Unfortunately for Johnny's precious Honda, there wasn't enough left of it to drive, Miguel having forced Shirlee off the road and into a tree in the woods. It was smashed beyond repair. Transporting Rog was difficult, still in a heavy cast, but between Johnny, Perry and Gonzalez, they had carried and maneuvered him into the back seat of one of the police sedans, into a motel room and back into the car this morning. With Gonzalez at the wheel, White alongside and Rog wedged in the back, he followed Lapidus, the two police cars now heading down the mountain toward Los Angeles.

"You should still be careful, Watson," said Lapidus. "That Reyes is dangerous. I don't know if he's still gunning for you and Rog and we have an APB out for him, but stay alert."

"We should get a search warrant for the house in East L.A.," said Perry, riding in the passenger seat up front. "Who knows what he and Lopez were into there."

"Right. And we know he has some connection to the Whiskey," said Lapidus. "We should look into the records of the place. But my guess is whatever is happening there is way off the books."

"It's probably drugs," opined Johnny. "You know, music clubs and drugs kinda go hand in hand." He didn't want to say the obvious, that their friend in the back seat of the other car had one of those hands in the club's drug trade for years.

"Maybe," said Lapidus. "But I think it's something more. A business like that, a lot of money flows through there every night. And a guy like Reyes probably has a piece of a lot of pies."

"Zzzzz." The police radio on the dashboard belched static and a voice came through. "Car one, this is two, over." It was White's voice. Perry picked up the handheld device.

"Yeah, Detective," answered Perry. "What's up?"

"We have a request here from our stretched out passenger in the back. Insists on talking to Watson."

Perry looked back at Johnny who shrugged his shoulders. Perry shook his head, in resigned disbelief.

"All right. Put him on." Perry handed the hand held to Johnny.

Fifteen seconds of clanking and audible fumbling were followed by Rog's voice.

"Johnny, mate. You there?"

"Yeah, Rog. I'm here." He smiled at Shirlee. Where else would he be?

"Good, mate, good. Listen, I wanna tell ya that if I ever get back to managing the Whiskey, or any other place in town, or any other place anywhere, you know, here or in New York, San Fran, or even London or Paris, or Rome or Moscow…"

"Rog, we don't need a travelogue."

"Right, right. Jus sayin that you guys are my prime act, okay. Conflict can play whenever ya wanna. And I'll get you some prime slot. Openers for big acts. Okay?"

"Sounds great, Rog."

"Yeah, well, after all you've done for me, you know, it's the least I can do."

"Thanks, Rog. So that means you'll pay me the five thousand dollars you promised?"

"Well, now, ya really din't find out what happened there, didja?"

Groans erupted from the backseat of Lapidus' car.

"All right, all right," said Rog hastily. "I know I owe ya. Hey, can I drink in the back seat of a police car? I mean, I'm a guest, right? Not under arrest and all. I have me a little bottle of gin here."

Now laughter erupted from Gonzalez' car.

"Don't push it, Cray," said White. "Car two out." The line went silent.

"Quite a character," said Perry, as he reattached the handheld to the holder on the dashboard.

"Yeah, he is," said Johnny. He squeezed Shirlee's hand as he stared out the window. The trees thinned as the road curved. He wondered if they would ever play the Whiskey again. It had only been a couple of weeks since the blow up at Slim's but it felt like forever since he had the electric boost of having a band playing in, around and behind him. Playing the guitar by himself was fine but nothing replaced that uplifting feeling, that crackle of energy he got from playing with a group of people, especially in a group of like-minded players. He turned to Shirlee. "We've gotta play again. Soon."

She smiled, leaned over and kissed him on the cheek.

CHAPTER 43

It was early evening and the streetlights were on. Darkness had descended on Los Angeles when Miguel Reyes turned the pick-up onto La Verne Ave. He knew the house that Lopez had owned on paper but that he had paid for and controlled would be the first place the police would search once they came back into town. Everything had to be cleaned out of there or else he'd be finished. It was bad enough that he hadn't eliminated the kid and the Brit, two people linking him to the house and the club. If the cops got their hands on the stuff in the house, if they were able to use that as evidence, he'd be on the run forever. And knowing Paco, forever might not last too long.

He drove down the block and around the corner, and parked next to a vacant lot, exiting the car but leaving the engine running. He knew the area and the kids in the area. The sound of an engine running in one spot for more than a minute would attract attention. Finding an empty unlocked vehicle with the engine going was perfect for at least a joyride. He knew the car would be gone within minutes, which is what Reyes wanted.

Walking around the corner in the direction he had driven, it took him five minutes to reach Chuy's front door. He rang the bell, two quick jabs. No answer. He banged loudly.

"Chuy!" he yelled. "Chuy, open up." More banging.

"Whaaat?" he heard from within the house. Sounds of door chains being unlatched followed and the door opened an inch. An eye peered through the opening.

"Oh, Patrón, it's you." The door shut, two more door chains were removed and the door swung open. "Que pasa?" Chuy asked. He was wearing a long white tee shirt and loose fitting jeans.

Reyes didn't answer but pushed past Chuy into the entranceway of the house. "Shut the door," he said.

"Sure, sure," said Chuy, pushing the door shut and relocking the chains. "You wanna beer?"

"Maybe later. We've got work to do. Get your truck and pull it into the driveway 'cross the street. I'll meet you over there." The door chains came off again and Reyes opened the door, looked out into the street, saw no traffic and ran to the front door of the Lopez house. He punched in the code on the numeric lock and entered. Piles of thick envelopes were just inside the front door and Reyes scooped them up, placing them in a box he found in the front room and carrying it with him. The house was sparsely furnished. A table and couch in the living room with nothing on the walls except a thirty inch TV. A barebones kitchen that looked like no one had ever cooked in it. The two bedrooms down the hall were identically furnished, each with a single bed, a nightstand and a lamp. Without Sylvia around, there was no activity and the house was empty of people. Just the way he wanted it right now.

He extracted a key from his pants pocket and opened the lock on the screen door, pushing it open along the tracks, leading into the backyard. Cardboard boxes were stacked in rows, three boxes high, a dozen stacks. Miguel opened the gate separating the backyard from the driveway, keyed in another combination on the numeric lock on the gate and opened it. He let in Chuy who had been waiting, standing in the driveway alongside a late edition silver Ford-150 truck.

"Come on," Miguel said. "We're gonna move all these boxes into your place tonight. This house is too hot."

They spent the next hour hauling the heavy boxes from the backyard to the bed of the truck, driving it across the street, stacking the boxes in the living room of Chuy's house and then repeating the process until the backyard was empty. Before leaving the Lopez house, Miguel unlocked the door to a garage at the far end of the backyard. Inside was a folding table around which were four chairs and on top of which was a money counting machine. Miguel tucked the machine under his arm, left the shed and then the house, locking all the doors as he exited.

"I'll have that cerveza now," he said to Chuy, after stacking the last box in Chuy's front room. Chuy disappeared into the kitchen and returned carrying a six pack of Dos Equis. Miguel took one, unscrewed the cap and took a deep drink.

"Now what?" asked Chuy, looking over his living room now turned into a warehouse.

"Tomorrow we unload all this. As fast as possible."

ON THE OTHER SIDE OF TOWN, IN THE SAN FERNANDO Valley town of Reseda, two couples were having a reunion. Billy shoved a joint into Johnny's hand as soon as he stepped into the apartment. Olivia rushed to embrace Shirlee.

"My god, mahn," said Billy. "This is the craziest week ever. You two okay?"

"Yeah," said Johnny, inhaling a stream of smoke. "That was too close though." He told Billy and Olivia what had transpired at the cabin in Lake Arrowhead, the gunfight, the task force arriving and Miguel disappearing. "The cops were going to drop Rog back at his place in Hollywood. I told him I'd come by tomorrow."

"Cool," said Billy. "I got a new song for us. Wanna hear?" He didn't wait for the response and got his acoustic guitar out of the bedroom, an Epiphone that was scratched and pock-marked from years of use but sounded fine. He strummed a C chord with a slow, steady rhythm and sang,

"Where was I without you

"Wandered long, I wandered long

"Never knew what I could do

"Never knew who I could be

"Whooooo, I could be

"Only you, only you

"Without you, what would I be

"Only you, only you, only you…"

"Bet Olivia likes that one," interrupted Johnny. "For walking down the aisle?"

"Maybe," said Billy, smiling crookedly at Olivia.

"Anybody hungry?" asked Shirlee, breaking the atmosphere. "Employee discount at Norm's?"

"Pancakes?" said Billy, excitedly changing gears. "I'll drive." They exited the apartment, all four of them together for what seemed to Johnny to be the first time in ages, although it was less than a couple of weeks.

CHAPTER 50

The next day was bright and sunny, a typical Southern California day, as Johnny drove into Hollywood, Olivia in the passenger seat dressed in a skirt and blouse, ready for work. After feasting on pancakes and celebrating Olivia's and Billy's engagement and Johnny and Shirlee escaping their mountain vacation with their lives the night before, the two couples retired to the apartment and an early night's sleep. That morning, Billy drove the Subaru to the Active store. Olivia told Johnny he could use her aunt's car for now if he would drop her off at work.

Johnny made a left off Melrose Avenue toward the Paramount gate and Olivia opened the door to exit.

"Thanks for the ride," she said. "I'll Uber home." She shut the car door, showed her employee pass to the guard in the booth and walked through the pedestrian entrance on the right.

Johnny made a U-turn out of the entrance and went west the short distance to Rog's apartment. He parked on the street and pressed the buzzer on the apartment house entrance. No answer. He buzzed again. No answer. Shit, he thought, not again. He jabbed at the button three times in quick succession, no longer expecting a response. He paused, wondering if he should press all the other apartment buttons at once, or just a few at a time, when the door buzzed. He pulled open the door and ascended the stairs through the door on his right, exiting the staircase on the second floor. The door to Rog's apartment was open. Alarms went off in Johnny's head. He reached for his gun usually in his shoulder holster, forgetting that he wasn't going to work today and had left the gun in the glove compartment of the car. He slowly inched forward and peered through the two inch opening but couldn't see anything.

"Rog?" he called out, tensing, his body and mind at high alert. "Rog, you there?"

Again no answer for what felt like hours but in reality was only a minute. Johnny took a deep breath and began to inch the door open with his foot.

"Hold it right there," came Rog's voice from inside. "Another step and I'll blow ya freakin head off."

"Rog, man," said Johnny. "It's me, Johnny."

"Watson? That you?" asked a relieved Rog. "Oh hell. Come in."

Johnny stepped in. Rog was standing on crutches, a shotgun lowered toward the floor in one arm.

"Expecting an invasion?" Johnny asked.

"Don't joke. Not after what we've been through." He lowered the shotgun on the couch and hopped-walked to the kitchen. "Coffee?"

Johnny sank into an overstuffed chair in the dining room, then reached underneath himself to extract a pile of magazines and papers. "I'm good. You should clean this place up."

"Yeah. I guess we made a mess of it." He stopped pouring water into the sieve and turned to Johnny. "I can't believe it. I thought we really had something. I guess I'm just an old fool."

"Rog, you were hurting and a beautiful woman showed you kindness and love. Easy to be turned around by that. To be a fool for love."

"Like the song, right?" He finished pouring water, waited for it to drain through the coffee into the mug and joined Johnny in the living room.

"So what's next for you?" Johnny asked.

"Don't know." Rog sipped his coffee. "Ya know, the club was my life for the past few years. We should go over there tonight. See what's goin on."

"Is that such a good idea? You don't want your other leg shattered."

"I'd have a matched set then."

Johnny's phone rang. "Hello?" he answered.

"Watson. It's Detective Lapidus. How are you?"

"Good, Detective. What's up?"

"I wanted you to know that we searched Lopez' house on La Verne this morning and found nothing. Place had been cleaned out. And no one's there. Perry and I knocked on the door across the street, at Chuy's place, but no one answered."

"Can't you get a warrant? You know he's mixed up with Miguel and his gang."

"Being an associate with a wanted criminal is not enough probable cause to get a warrant. Just keep an eye out. No one's spotted Reyes yet. I don't think he'd be foolish enough to take another crack at you or Cray but you never know."

"All right. Okay, Detective. I'm with Rog now. I'll let him know." Rog gave him a questioning look. Johnny held up his hand, index finger up, indicating he'd tell him in a minute.

"Okay. Remember, watch yourself." The phone went dead and Johnny put it aside.

"Lapidus?" asked Rog. "What'd she say?"

"That we should watch our asses cause there's been no sign of Miguel. She doesn't think he'll try anything. But you know what they say, when people are backed into a corner…"

"Yeah," interrupted Rog. "That's when they're most dangerous. Sheesh, I am so tired of this shite. Let's go to the club tonight. Get a drink, hassle the crap outta Les. Whaddya say?"

"I say you're fucked up. But all right. Can you manage a ride? I'll meet you out front around 9:30." Johnny stood to leave.

"Yeah. Sure. Great," said Rog. "Thanks, bro. I need a little clear-headed fun."

"Okay. Later." Johnny walked out of the apartment, leaving Rog to his coffee and late morning TV shows. There was no real reason to go to the Whiskey, he thought. They could go out to a bar within a few blocks of his apartment. Unless Rog has something else in mind. He punched a speed dial number on his phone as he walked out of the apartment building into the noonday sun.

"Billy. What time do you get off work? You wanna go with me to the Whiskey tonight? Cool. Meet you back at your place then." He disconnected. It was a beautiful day for taking a walk down Hollywood Boulevard, he thought. He left the car on Fountain and walked north.

CHAPTER 51

"It's time. Get in the truck." The sweat dripped off Chuy's forehead as he shoved the last of the boxes in the bed of the Ford 150 and fastened the tarp over it. It had been over an hour to load, with Miguel's nephew acting as lookout, watching surreptitiously out of a corner of the front window, keeping the lights off in the living room. The sky had turned dark and the first stars were becoming visible.

Miguel and Chuy had watched earlier that morning when the cops smashed down the front door to Lopez' house, only to emerge an hour later with nothing, just as Miguel had planned. When the big black cop rang Chuy's bell, they had hid quietly in the bedroom, knowing that the police didn't have a warrant and hoping that they wouldn't break in anyway. They hadn't. But after hearing cars drive off, Miguel saw that they had left one cop sitting in a Crown Vic parked in Lopez' driveway, watching Chuy's house. Any movement would be noticed.

But Miguel knew that getting the contents of the boxes out and distributed was more than essential. Everything was hanging on it. He called his nephew, Roberto, and instructed him to come to the house. An hour later, he had arrived in a '76 silver Dodge Charger, the engine roaring as he pulled into the driveway. Miguel had unlocked the door and Roberto had pretended to use a key and entered the house. For the last hour he had been stationed in the front, eyeing the cop as the cop was eyeing the house, while Miguel and Chuy emptied the living room of boxes into the truck parked behind a gate in the driveway. Now they needed a diversion.

"Bobby," called Miguel. "This is what I need you to do." He handed his nephew an empty cardboard box. "Fill this up with newspapers, magazines, give it weight. Take it out to your car and make sure the cop sees you. Then drive away. Not fast. Then just drive east for an hour. Then you can go home. Hopefully the cop will follow you. If he stops you, you know what to do and say."

"Nothin'," said Roberto, smiling, happy to be in on his favorite uncle's plans. He admired his mother's ruthless brother, how he maintained a grip on his people, took care of business and never had to worry about the rent or grocery bills. Although only seventeen, he was already moving up, he thought. Whatever Miguel needed, he'd supply. He took one last look at the cop still wearing sunglasses behind the wheel of the Crown Vic across the street, then began filling the box.

Roberto lifted the now heavy box, identical from the exterior to the boxes that were once in Lopez' backyard and now sat in the bed of the F-150 in the driveway. He went through the front door, put the box in the trunk of the Dodge, started the engine and drove toward the freeway entrance.

Miguel watched from the window. He saw the cop speaking on the two-way radio when Bobby had walked out of the house. Now he drove the car onto the street, following the Dodge. Perfect, thought Miguel.

He hurried back through the house, out the back door and jumped in the truck next to Chuy.

"Give it ten minutes." That should be enough time for Bobby and the cop to both get clear of the area. They'd be halfway to Norwalk by then.

Chuy put the radio on KTWV, the station playing "Bailamos", Enrique Iglesias' vocals ringing out. Chuy sang along.

"Bailamos. Te quiero amor mio, bailamos…"

"Hey, Chuy," interrupted Miguel. "Less singing, more driving."

Oh, si Patrón. Where we goin?"

"West Hollywood. Take the 10 west to the 101. We're gonna have Les live up to his end of the deal."

While Chuy headed west, Detective Gonzalez was going east, following the kid in the Dodge Charger. He hadn't seen the kid before but called him in to Lapidus when he first showed up at Chuy's house. There was no record of Miguel having a kid, but his sister, Bonita, had four and one boy was the right age, 17.

He had seen the kid carrying one box into his car. It looked like the boxes from Lopez' backyard, but it was impossible to tell. If it was part of those boxes, where were the others? In Chuy's house? And where the hell was the kid going? Out to Riverside to offload drugs?

The Dodge ahead of him was going nice and steady, doing an even sixty-five in the second lane, even as other cars were passing him on the right doing seventy and on the left at speeds Gonzalez estimated were above eighty. Work for the California Highway Patrol, he thought. Traffic had eased this late at night, the rush hour over, just the normal flow of cars ahead. He picked up his two-way radio and pressed the button.

"Lapidus, you there?"

Static and then Lapidus' voice crackled through. "I'm here, Detective. What's your 10-40?"

"Passing the 605. Baldwin Park. Deep in the San Gabriel Valley now and steadily heading east."

"You've been on him for half an hour now."

"Roger. Starting to feel like I'm being yanked like a dog on a leash. No evasive movement. Obeying the speed limit. Not at all like a seventeen year old."

"You're right, Gonzalez. This smells bad. Break off. Come back to Hollywood."

"Roger. Out." He clicked the hand held back on the hook and looked for the next exit. He drove down the off ramp, turned left, then left again onto the ramp and freeway heading west, retracing his route.

CHAPTER 52

"You know," said Johnny. "This place has become our home away from home, hasn't it?"

"Ya mahn," agreed Billy, looking up at the Whiskey marquee on the corner of Sunset and Clark. "But when we get to play here again? Or play anywhere for dat matta?"

It was close to nine at night and Johnny had picked Billy up at his place in Reseda after he had gotten home from work. After stopping for a quick meal at an In-N-Out on Van Nuys Boulevard, they drove into Hollywood. Now they watched cars stopping by the curb, discharging their passengers, eager for a night of music and fun. So far, no Rog.

Shirlee was at work at the Norm's, donning her waitress outfit that Johnny thought was cute as hell on her. The fact that it was usually stained with gravy, grease and sweat didn't really bother him. But it was just as well she wasn't here tonight, he thought. Who knows what'll go down between Les and his biker friends and Rog. Johnny had his .32 in the back of his waistband. After everything that had gone down, he wanted the added protection. But he had to admit he was getting tired of acting as combination bodyguard and sleuth. Billy was right. They had strayed pretty far from their natural and preferred vocations of being musicians.

"Hi guys."

"Livie! Whad'r'ya doin here?" asked Billy, exasperation in his voice. She had stepped out of a Toyota Corolla Uber that neither Billy nor Johnny had paid attention to, the vehicle not being large enough to transport the cast-dragging Rog. "I thought we agreed that I'd see you at home later?"

"And miss out on all the action? Shirlee told me how terrifying and exciting it was at the cabin. Maybe they'll be a shoot out on the Sunset Strip tonight!"

"That's what we need," said Johnny facetiously.

"You be crazy, baby," said Billy, grabbing her around the waist. "But I'm glad to see you." They embraced and kissed, unmindful of the crowd around them filing into the club.

"Hey, you two kids, break it up." A Toyota SUV had pulled to the curb and a familiar head poked out of the back seat window.

"You shouldn't give anybody advice about love, Mr. Brit Advice to the Lovelorn," said Johnny, opening the passenger door and helping Rog out, first crutches, then legs, then the rest of his considerable frame.

"Ah, it's good to be back," said Rog, looking up and down the street at the small crowd gathering outside the club, and looking up at the marquee. "But who the hell are 'The Young Men' and 'Soul Times 2'?"

"Your new fav bands," said Olivia, taking one of Rog's arms and leading him toward the entrance, Johnny and Billy following close behind.

"Oh no! He comes trouble." Tim, the big, no-nonsense Samoan bouncer at the front door saw Rog and threw restraint to the wind. "You motherfucker." He embraced Rog, crutches and all. "How the fuck have you been?"

"Me?" said Rog. "Doin great, can't ya tell? Got me own entourage and groupie wit me."

"Hey, don't be pushin it," cautioned Billy, taking mock offense on Olivia's behalf.

"Yeah. The white rasta gonna bring hellfire down on you," Tim joked. "Go on, on me tonight." He stamped the right hands and wrists of Rog, Johnny, Billy and Olivia and ushered them into the club.

A sign on the stage said "The Young Men." Three men, none younger than fifty, were hammering away at Howlin' Wolf's "I'm a Man" as if the sixties had never ended. After watching for a minute, Billy and Olivia walked over to the bar to get a couple of drinks from Vibes.

"Let's use the elevator in back," Rog said. "I don't think I can manage the stairs." Johnny followed him as he went through a partially hidden doorway to an alcove in the back of the club. Rog inserted a key that he had in his pocket, turned it and pressed the single button. They heard the sounds of a moving elevator, which opened a moment later.

Ten minutes before they headed upstairs, a Ford 150 was turning up Clark Street off Sunset and making a left into the alley, stopping near the back door of the club.

"Hey boss," said the parking attendant at the adjacent lot. "You can't park in the alley."

Chuy waved the attendant over and handed him a twenty dollar bill. "We won't be long." The attendant nodded and walked back to the cars waiting to park in the lot.

"Stay here," said Miguel. "I'll talk to Les. Then we'll unload these cartons in the basement." He exited the vehicle and entered the club through the back door. It was dark inside and Miguel could barely make out a figure sitting at the end of the small hallway. As he approached, Miguel could see that the big man looked familiar. Biker jeans jacket with "Death Playas" logo on the back. One of Del's guys.

"Hello Smokey," he said, getting within two feet of the biker. Smokey turned around, his attention having been on the floor of the club.

"Who's that?" He squinted and hunched his shoulders, trying to see through the darkness. "That you, Miguel?"

"Si, hombre. Listen. I'm gonna talk to Les upstairs. Be down in a few minutes. Then I need you to help Chuy out back with some packages, okay?"

"Sure, sure. I'll be here." They fist bumped and Miguel walked onto the floor of the club, turned and walked up the stairs to the second floor.

CHAPTER 53

The crowd was sparse upstairs. Two couples were sitting at a table by the railing, watching the blues band playing down on the stage, and a waitress, short skirt, tee shirt, bored faraway eyes, taking the couples' drink orders, had the entire floor to themselves. Reyes noticed and ignored them, proceeding up the second and shorter staircase to the door of the office. He knocked once and then opened the door.

"Hey! Who the hell…" Les' squeaky yell greeted Miguel. It took a moment for him to recognize his visitor. "Miguel. Hey, how are you, man. Good to see you. Macey, run along now."

The blonde teenage girl looked Miguel over from head to toe as she made her way from Les' lap and out the door.

Miguel shut and locked the door behind her. Les sat in his armchair behind the desk, swarmed under by the stacks of rock and roll memorabilia on the desk and on the walls surrounding him. Gold and platinum albums by the Doors, Van Halen, The Byrds. Autographed pictures of Johnny Rivers, Bruce Springsteen, Dr. John, X. A Devo hat signed by the group. A baseball signed by John Fogerty. Miguel looked the stuff over and thought he could make a small fortune on Ebay selling this stuff to baby boomers.

"You like this stuff?" asked Les. "You wouldn't believe what they have in storage in this place. Found all this just rummaging around one day. Wild, huh?"

"Yeah. Sure," said Miguel. "What's the situation with our business?" he said abruptly, cutting off all other thoughts in Les' head.

"Yeah, good, man. Doin good," Les said, trying to reassure him.

"You've swept up everything I gave you so far?"

"Yeah. Took a few more days than I thought. Like I said before, I can only do so much at a time. Depends on how many people show."

"You're gonna have to work harder at it."

"But Miguel…"

Miguel came around the desk, grabbed Les by the shirt collar and lifted him out of his chair.

"Listen, amigo," Miguel said, his face inches from Les'. "You wouldn't have your sweet little job, with your little groupies and music trash to play with, without me. You get your salary plus a piece of my drug action for taking care of my shit. If you can't handle it, you're easily replaceable." He pushed Les back into his seat, the chair rolling a few inches backward.

"Miguel, please," pleaded Les. "I can't shove more cash through the place. The owners will catch on and we'll have the Feds down our necks."

"I don't care!" yelled Miguel. He took two steps toward Les and smashed a backhand fist to Les' face. He tumbled out of the chair onto the floor, blood spilling from his nose. Miguel stood over him. "I'm putting 20 boxes in your storage room downstairs. Get rid of the contents in the next two weeks. If you don't, you won't have to worry about a new job. Comprende?" Les wagged his head and a splash of sweat and blood fell to the floor. "Good."

Miguel picked up the Devo hat and threw it at Les, who shielded himself with his hands. Miguel turned and opened the door and said "Two weeks" in admonition to Les and left, leaving the door ajar. He headed down the stairs and toward the back door. Strange, he thought. Where was Smokey? He was gonna need him to move those boxes.

Miguel stepped outside and saw Smokey. He was standing next to the pick-up with Chuy laying in a puddle of blood at his feet in the alleyway, his throat slit. A gun was in Smokey's hand and it was pointed at Miguel. "Paco sends his regards," Smokey said.

Moments prior as Miguel had stepped onto the stage floor, Rog and Johnny were exiting the elevator. The alcove on the third floor led directly to the office. Johnny knocked on the door, then knocked twice more when there was no answer.

"What?" Les voice came through the door. Johnny opened it and he and Rog walked in, finding Les picking himself up off the floor.

"What happened to you, mate?" asked Rog, seeing that Les' nose was bleeding and his eyes were beginning to swell.

"Miguel," croaked Les, fighting back tears. "Fuckin Miguel."

"Miguel?!" exclaimed Johnny. "He was here?"

"Yeah, he was here," said Les, settling into his chair and wiping his face with his shirtsleeve. "Asshole left just a minute ago."

Johnny burst out of the office door and ran down the short staircase. At the top of the stairs on the second floor, he scanned the room, looking for Miguel in the crowd.

Nothing. He ran down the stairs two at a time, surveyed the room again, then ran down the hall. No one was there.

As he touched the back door, he heard a gunshot outside. He pushed through in time to see a Ford pickup speeding down the alley and making a screeching right onto the street. Another screeching sound followed.

On the ground were two bodies. Johnny recognized the guy from La Verne Street, now lying dead in a pool of blood. And Johnny knew he finally caught up with Miguel, who was laying on his back, his hands over a hole in his chest, which was spurting blood. His lips moved silently as he tried to talk to Johnny, who bent over him, his ear to Miguel's lips. A whisper of air floated up along with drops of red blood but no intelligible words. Then Miguel's eyes went blank.

CHAPTER 54

Hours later, Detective White was wrapping up the on-scene investigation and speaking with Lapidus, Gonzalez and Perez, all of whom were alerted to the crime scene. The coroner had been called in and the bodies of Chuy and Miguel had been taken away.

Vibes, Tim, Johnny, Billy, Rog, and Olivia, huddled together, were standing to the side against the back wall of the club, waiting to be told they could go. Each had spoken to the police and given what information they had. The rest of the night's patrons had already been dismissed. Les was in the back seat of a patrol car, waiting to be processed at the West Hollywood Station.

"According to the manager, Lester Powell, Reyes had threatened him with physical harm or worse," said White. "Insisted that if he didn't launder money for him, he was a dead man. Admitted outright to money laundering."

"Where's the evidence?" asked Lapidus.

"We'll look at the club's books. But other than that, there is none. No cash," said White. "Watson said he saw a Ford pickup speeding away from the scene. Maybe with the evidence. Maybe with those boxes from Lopez' house. Watson caught a glimpse of some big long-haired guy driving the pickup. Could be one of the bikers who were always hanging around."

"Maybe," said Gonzalez. "The bartender, Victor Krassley, aka 'Vibes', said only a biker named Smokey was working tonight. And he's nowhere to be found."

"He's one of the Death Playas, right?" asked Perez. White nodded affirmatively. "We can make a visit to their hang-out 'The Hungry One' above Pasadena and see if we find him there. But odds are he's in Mexico already. With whatever evidence might have been in the truck."

"You're probably right. We put out an APB a couple of hours ago on the Ford truck and a long-haired male driver," said White. "But so far nothing."

"Okay," said Lapidus. "There's nothing more to do here. Let's break for the night and meet at the Hollywood Station in the morning." The four detectives dispersed and Gonzalez walked over to Johnny.

"You okay?" he asked. Johnny nodded his reply. "You know you're fortunate. If you had come through that door a minute earlier, you might not be standing here."

"I know," said Johnny.

"Mahn, you livin lucky," said Billy. "The bank robbery, the cabin shoot out and now this?"

Johnny's phone rang.

"Hello?" he answered.

"Johnny? It's Charles. Shirlee gave me your number." He was gasping for air. "Watch out tonight. I had a dream just now that it was raining bullets all around you."

"Ha. Your dreams are coming a little late now, Charles. Don't worry. I'm fine." Johnny disconnected the line without explaining.

"Okay then," said Gonzalez, shaking Johnny's hand. "Take it easy. You know, if you ever think of becoming a cop, let me know. You'd make a good candidate."

"What?!" cried Billy. "Johnny Whoops a cop? Oh that's so non rock n roll."

Johnny laughed. "I think Billy's right, Detective. But thanks for the compliment." He turned to Rog. "Need a lift home?"

"Yeah, sure. Just give me a minute, wudja?" Rog walked over haltingly on his crutches to Vibes and Tim. "Hey, mates. Everybody good?" They bumped fists all around. "So now that Les is, er, preoccupied, I'm gonna give the owner a call. Even with crutches I think I can do the job here. You guys with me?"

"Yeah man," said Tim. "Talk to Marv. Even you again would be better than that guy was," he joked.

"Right on, man. We're with ya," said Vibes.

"Okay, good t'hear. I'll see ya soon." Rog caught up with Johnny, Billy and Olivia at the Kia parked on Sunset. "Can ya squeeze me in there?"

"You take the back seat," said Olivia, opening the back door and stepping onto the sidewalk. "I'll double up with Billy." She opened the front passenger door and settled onto Billy's lap, while Rog moved in stages into the back seat.

"Hmm, comfy," said Billy as he nuzzled Olivia's neck.

"Everybody in?" asked Johnny. "Okay, next stop Hollywood." He pulled out from the curb, made a U-turn in the middle of Sunset Boulevard and headed east.

"Whoa, mahn," said Billy. "You be gettin a ticket."

"Aw, don't think so," said Johnny. "I know some cops." He turned on the radio and sang along to Tom Petty's recording of "Free Fallin'" as they headed into the night.

CHAPTER 55

A month later, Billy and Olivia stepped out of a black stretch limousine onto the curb outside the Whiskey. He was wearing a white tuxedo, complete with tails and a white top hat, she in a white lace gown, with enough frills to satisfy any fashion designer on either coast.

"Watch your step, Mrs. Bates," Billy said as he took Olivia's hand.

"Well, thank you, Mr. Bates," Olivia replied, bowing as if they were in an English period piece movie. Then they both burst out laughing.

"Hey, watch it, you two," a voice with a British accent said behind them on the street. "Can't have all the fun out here."

"Hey, Rog!" shouted Billy. He reached out and gave Rog a bear hug.

"Hey rasta boy, ya gonna knock over me cane," said Rog. He had progressed in his healing and had been able to lose the crutches just days before. "Come on in, newlyweds. The joint is all set up for ya."

Olivia and Billy followed Rog inside the Whiskey. They passed Big Tim at the door who kissed Olivia on the cheek and gave Billy a soul handshake and a hug.

The entrance to the club was as dark as ever, but as soon as they turned the corner onto the stage floor, they were nearly blinded. A spot light was shining on a sheet draped on the wall behind the stage that read "Congratulations Billy and Olivia!"

They had made it official earlier that day. The couple, along with witnesses Johnny and Shirlee, had gone downtown to City Hall, paperwork and rings in hand. They impatiently stood in line with the other couples and friends but a half hour later the civil ceremony was complete. The four friends had spent the afternoon partying in Griffith Park, drinking champagne and smoking weed, the boys taking turns playing songs on Johnny's acoustic guitar with everyone singing, hiking up the hill to the site of the original, now abandoned zoo, looking down at the city from the observatory. As the sun set, they went back to their respective apartments to get ready for the big night.

"That is so wonderful!" said Olivia, taking in the hanging message. She hugged Rog again.

"There you guys are." Johnny emerged from the shadows near the bar, Shirlee beside him and Vibes a step behind. They all embraced.

"Everybody to the bar," insisted Vibes. "Who wants what?" He scooted behind the bar and began making the called-out orders, vodka and cranberry, scotch and soda, rum and coke, and quite a few beers.

"To Billy and Olivia!" shouted Vibes.

"To Billy and Olivia!" came the shouted response.

On stage, four musicians, a guitarist, keyboard player, bass player and drummer, were setting up. Charles came to the front of the stage. He was wearing a jumpsuit with horizontal black and white stripes. He spoke into the mic.

"Hi."

"Hi Charles," yelled Shirlee.

"Hi Shirl," said Charles. "I want to thank you all for inviting me here and for letting me debut my new band 'The Secret Dream.' You ready?" he asked the four musicians behind him. "Okay then. Benny, let's go."

The drummer counted "1, 2…" and the guitarist started playing a halting guitar phrase. The rest of the band joined in and Charles began to sing in a squeaky tenor.

"I, I, I, have a secret…"

"I, I, I, have a secret…"

"I think he has a secret," a female voice said, approaching the knot of people by the bar. Lapidus was dressed in jeans, cowboy boots and a black western shirt. Perry next to her was wearing a pinstriped suit.

"Detectives!" said Billy. "Glad you could make it. Vibes, set em up for L.A.'s finest."

"What about Beverly Hills' finest?"

"Or West Hollywood's finest?"

Gonzalez and White joined the group, all congratulating the happy couple and grabbing drinks.

Charles' band played on, providing a backdrop for dancing, drinking and mingling.

"So, Detective," Johnny said to Lapidus as they watched Billy spin Olivia around the dance floor. "Ever find Smokey?"

"No. We had an ABP for him and alerted border patrol but we never found him. And of course everyone at The Hungry One claims he disappeared off the face of the earth. Actually their leader, Del, was really pissed. Like Smokey had betrayed him, chosen a Mexican drug dealer over the brotherhood."

"Is that what happened? A Mexican drug dealer was responsible for Miguel's and the other guy's death?"

"We don't know for sure. But Reyes was after you and

Rog probably because he needed to operate here without any problems. We know that the guy you shot in Lake Arrowhead was one of the men in the car who shot at me and Perry on the freeway. And he was also involved in the bank robbery in Beverly Hills. It was all connected. And if those boxes that were in the back of the pickup contained cash, Reyes was probably trying to launder it through the club. We know Sureños 13 has connections to a cartel operating out of Juarez. So the pieces don't all fit, but they come close. But without evidence…" Lapidus shrugged her shoulders.

"What about Les?" asked Johnny.

Lapidus snorted a rueful laugh. "Him? Pretty useless. I don't think anyone told him anything except that he had to make cash disappear."

"Come on, Johnny," said Olivia, interrupting the conversation, her wedding dress now reduced to a skirt and blouse. "Let's play."

"Okay, okay." He took her hand and grabbed Billy around the shoulders as they walked up the stairs at the back of the stage. "Where's Frankie?"

"Here I come," Frank called, running down the stairs from the second floor, where he had been entertaining and been entertained by a tall, thin, dark haired young girl.

They all took their places on the stage, Frank in the corner with his bass, Olivia behind the drums, Billy holding his guitar and tapping one of his pedals with his foot and Johnny adjusting the mic to the proper height.

"Excuse me," he said into the mic. "Excuse me." The room grew quiet. "Hi. Welcome everybody. Before we begin, I want to thank Rog for offering the famous Whiskey to us for the night and for picking up the tab. Cheers, mate," he said in an English accent. "We're all glad you're back with all your people where you belong. I also want to thank everyone who is here, our people, for coming out on this glorious night to celebrate the wedding of my best bud Billy…" The crowd cheered and Billy took a bow. "…and the second most beautiful girl in L.A…" he winked at Shirlee, standing at the lip of the stage. "…Olivia!" She stood up behind the drums and waved her hands at the crowd. "All right now. Ready to rock? Count it off Mrs. Bates."

Oliva clicked her drum sticks and said "…2, 3, 4…' the band kicked in and Johnny sang.

"Can you believe it
"Heaven is all around
"Can you believe it
"What's been lost is found
"Without another word
"Every thought is heard
"Oh my, what a glorious day.
"What a glorious, what a glorious day,
"Oh my, what a glorious day…"

THE END

The first book in the Conflict series,
Conflict in the City, is available in paperbook,
as an ebook and as an audiobook.
And look for the next book in the series
Conflict Up the Coast, coming soon.

Visit the author's website at philcohen-la.com.
Leave a comment, a review or just say hi.
You can also email the author at
philcohen.la@gmail.com.

www.ingramcontent.com/pod-product-compliance
Lightning Source LLC
LaVergne TN
LVHW041701060526
838201LV00043B/521